QUARTERBACK KEEPER

A COLLEGE SPORTS ROMANCE

FALL LAKE BALLERS
BOOK ONE

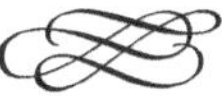

ISLA VAUGHN

ARROWSCOPE PRESS, LLC

Quarterback Keeper

(p) **ISBN-13**: 978-1-951919-67-2

(e) **ISBN-13**: 978-1-951919-66-5

Publisher: Arrowscope Press, LLC; www.arrowscopepress.com

Editing— Amanda K., Line Editor, Virge B., Proofreader, Rashida B., Beta Reader, Red Adept Editing

Cover Design—T.E. Black Designs; www.teblackdesigns.com

Interior Formatting & Design— Arrowscope Press, LLC; www.arrowscope-press.com

Collateral Damage

Rivals

Verretti Crime Family (coming soon)

Borrowed Time

My Enemy's Bed

Fractured Lies

Gray Ghost Novels (Former Navy SEALs)

Moments That Define Us

Broken Circle

Eye of the Storm

Beneath the Surface

Vantage Point

Covert Threat

Marked for Death

Deadly Isles Special Ops (Navy SEALs)

Twisted Secrets

Bound by Secrets

Forged by Secrets

Standalone Titles

Shattered Melody

Siren's Call: Cursed Seas

Fake Fiancé (A Second Chance Office Romance)

Moonlit Destination Series

Moonlit Whisper

Moonlit Kiss

Moonlit Mirage

Five Fates Series

Hidden

Taken

CHAPTER ONE

KYLIAN

"Mom." I crossed the college's parking lot, my phone pressed against my ear, headed for my SUV. "I can pick up food for dinner tonight. I'm leaving now."

"No need, Kylian." Mom's voice held a note of strain. "I'm on my way to the grocery store. I already know what I want to make for dinner, and you know how it goes. If I have a craving, I better act on it."

"Are you feeling okay?" I didn't like that she'd gone out so close to her last hospital treatment. Unlocking my SUV, I held open the back door, tensely waiting for her answer.

"I'm fine, but I'm driving. I'll see you at home."

I said goodbye then pocketed my phone. My backpack landed on the floorboard of my used Chevy Trailblazer with a thump. A bone-deep exhaustion had settled in after classes, the squeezing in of some homework, and a grueling practice. The day wasn't even close to over. On autopilot, I drove through rows of parked cars in the athletic lot before merging into traffic that would take me from Evanston to an up-and-coming area on the south side of Chicago. It took a little over an hour, not too long without traffic.

As I turned onto Mom's street, I got lucky and pulled into a parking spot half a block from the run-down building. My dad was a silent partner, but still a slumlord, for the building where Mom and I had lived until I moved out so I would be near campus. It was a point of contention between us and one I planned on bringing up again at dinner.

Movement caught my eye.

I turned and swore as I jumped out of the SUV, shoving my keys into the pocket of my athletic pants to free my hands. "Mom." I jogged to her as she slowly made her way from the CR-V I'd bought her to the front door of the four-story brownstone, a bag of groceries in her arms. I swooped in, relieved her of the heavy burden, and kissed her on the cheek then flashed a carefree smile that I hoped fooled her into thinking I wasn't in a shit mood.

I held the door, which also gave me time to study her. Her ordinarily shiny chestnut hair was dull and barely reached her shoulders, as it'd fallen out with the first round of chemo treatments that seemed a lifetime ago. New lines etched around her mouth but failed to steal the remnants of the vibrancy that clung to her—though I could tell she was tired. Stage four metastatic breast cancer would do that to a person.

As we climbed the stairs, she took my offered elbow rather than the railing, which had who knew what kind of germs.

"The condo next to mine is for sale. I want to put in an offer so you can move out of this dump. And it would be better if we lived in the same building. I could see you more."

Mom snorted. "You mean the dump you grew up in? Come on, Kylian. It's not that bad. We have lots of great memories here. And because of your father, I live here rent free."

The only good thing about the place was Mom's lack of rent. Still… "The elevator has been broken since I was in high school." I pushed my agenda, ignoring the dank, musty smell that'd clung to the stairwell for as long as I could remember. "You live on the fourth floor, and you can't tell me that's easy to climb after treatments."

"I'm glad it's broken." Her shoulders squared as she dug in her heels on the matter. "The exercise is good for me, and I see a lot more of you than I ever did when you were in high school. You bring me food and take me to doctor's visits."

"I would still do those things."

"Kyl, between your commitments with football and school, that broken elevator has given us time we wouldn't have had otherwise."

Ridiculous, but I couldn't deny it. Other than my mom, I lived for football. It was all I thought about and trained for, and I worked hard to be better than I was the day before. Last year, I even learned the defensive plays to get an edge on making quick decisions for the offensive line with the opposing team's defense.

"We have so many memories here," Mom said, pulling me from my thoughts. "And there are my friends. Mrs. Carlson in 2E and Fred in 4D with his cute little Chihuahua. Besides, I can picture the years ahead." She glanced at me, a calculating look in her tired deep-blue eyes. "With all the grandkids you're going to give me running up those stairs."

I didn't say a word. There was more to come. There always was, and it killed me that I couldn't give her what she craved most. I wouldn't.

"Football isn't your whole life. It's a part of it and might, someday, be a job. I want to see you get married and know that you have someone to care for and who will take care of you."

I clenched my fist, helplessness washing over me at her dreams I couldn't fulfill. "I don't need anyone, Mom. I've got you."

The sigh that pushed past her lips almost broke me. It said everything neither of us wanted to talk about. The doctor had been clear at the last appointment I'd gone to with her. She had months left, and that was if she was lucky and the experimental treatment plan worked.

On the final set of stairs, she squeezed my arm. "You've always been a good son."

I opened my mouth, but she shushed me. At her door, she fished for her keys, unlocked it, and let us inside.

"I know you work hard and think you have to make up for what your dad couldn't be for us, but that's unnecessary and unrealistic. That's not your burden. What I want most in my time left here is to see you happy."

And settled. She'd left out saying it, though she already had.

Mom shut the door behind us and flipped the deadbolt into place. I glanced around, noting the folded blanket on the couch where I knew she spent most of her recovery time after treatments. Everything about the apartment was tired, from the worn carpet that should've been ripped up and replaced with hardwood or vinyl years ago to the sagging furniture and lackluster kitchen. I set the grocery bag on the black-and-gray-spotted laminated counter, fighting another wave of anger at my dad and his business partners for refusing to update the building, specifically Mom's apartment. I'd tried to pay to have it done myself, but she'd refused.

I unpacked and put away the groceries, leaving out the bread, lettuce, and tomato. Mom got the bacon on a tray and slid it into the oven. We were having sandwiches for dinner. I waved off her apology because I didn't have much of an appetite with everything going on. After she set the timer, I urged her to sit on one of the kitchen chairs.

Her expression turned guarded, and she wrung her hands in her lap. "Has your father gotten ahold of you?"

"No, not recently." I didn't check, but I bet I had three missed calls or a few texts from him. I didn't care. Hatred bubbled under the tightly controlled expression I maintained for Mom's benefit. I wished with everything in me that he would leave us alone. "Why?" I both dreaded and needed to hear her reason for asking. Dad had always been more concerned about money and reputation to meddle too deeply with Mom and me—until recently. He wanted me, along with my football reputation, which was escalating to possible NFL status, to stand beside him as he kicked things off for his political aspirations. Fuck that.

"I'm not sure. Your father called trying to find you."

Annoyance ripped through me, and I sucked in air to stop my reaction. Mom didn't need that, and she was who I cared about. I would deal with him later—speak to him so she didn't have to. The less she knew about what he'd threatened me with, the better.

Mom had thought Dad was paying her medical bills, but I'd been covering her expenses until she'd discovered my part in the payments and the balance in my trust from Grandad passing away was almost gone—but I would figure it out. The plan was to complete my final year at Fall Lake University, but it might not be in the cards if I needed to come up with money to help Mom.

When I'd approached Dad about the bills for the new treatment, he'd only agreed to help if I did something for him. His ask was outrageous. The latest demand was that I date some contributor's daughter—he'd even hinted at me marrying her—during the campaign to keep the funds rolling in, and my father would pay for whatever Mom wanted or needed, including the twenty-thousand-dollar-apiece experimental treatments currently prolonging her life.

The more I thought about it, the less college seemed like a priority.

I chatted with Mom while we assembled the sandwiches and ate at the tiny two-person table in her small kitchen. My mind never strayed from the decisions I had to make. Money was a factor, and I would do anything for Mom. All I needed was a solid offer from a team in the league. Until then, I could stretch my remaining funds. I didn't care what I had to do.

I'd broached the idea of paying for her treatments with my money from Grandad, but Mom had put her foot down hard, threatening to stop them altogether if I did that. She kept track of all the invoices and insurance details. I couldn't sneak payments anymore without her finding out. That left one other option—Dad.

Her explanation was she didn't want to ruin my life. But she *was* my life.

It wasn't until I'd helped clean the kitchen, kissed her on her cheek, and closed the door behind me—waiting until I heard the bolt slide home, that I pulled my phone from my pocket. I had a text from Dad.

Hey, superstar. I saw you on ESPN last night. Call me. We need to talk.

Fury crackled and raced through my veins on the heels of the thinly veiled motivation in the text from dear old Dad. Even with a great evening with Mom, he managed to derail my mood. *Fuck him.*

My hands balled into fists as I rushed down the stairs and out the door of the brownstone. I knew what Dad's hollow congratulations meant—another attempt to use me for his power-hungry gain. With his narcissistic, overinflated ego, he had never cared about Mom or me, and with the increase in press coverage during football season, his demands had rolled in like clockwork.

ESPN's coverage last night had predicted Fall Lake U's QB1 —*me*—as a first-round pick in the upcoming NFL draft, if I entered it early and forwent my final year at school. I hadn't planned to because I'd promised Mom I would get my degree, and that was the smart thing to do. Accidents happened, derailing NFL careers before they even got started. But that was before the latest round of bills. With her escalating costs, my decision continued to waver.

Based on Dad's latest text, he'd heard ESPN's prediction. He should've known better. But he didn't. That would require listening and giving a shit about Mom and me.

His current obsession and single-minded ambition was to advance from being one of five Republicans running for Illinois State Senate to the primary election by any means necessary. His new blond bimbo of a wife was step one. I was step two—to use his football-phenom son, heralded as the next Tom Brady, to stand beside him as he kicked off his campaign. The thought of hobnobbing with one-percenters who manipulated the political scene made my stomach cramp. It wasn't my thing. It hadn't been Mom's either. Which was why everything had changed.

I unlocked my SUV with the key fob and threw myself inside. The weight resting on my shoulders continued to increase. My family both wanted and needed something from me, and time quickly fell through my grasp. My dad wanted to use me. My mom was dying, and I couldn't save her. Both wanted me to marry but for entirely different reasons.

The only thing I wanted was for my mom to live. *Marriage?* I'd survived my parents' toxic relationship and bitter divorce to know I didn't ever want to be legally tied to another person— not in the name of love or for my dad's political gain.

I leaned my head against the headrest and contemplated going home, where I lived with my two best friends, who were also my teammates. They'd had my back more times than I wanted to admit—even running interference with my dad when they sensed I was about to blow up in front of a stadium full of people and a slew of reporters waiting to catch anything newsworthy about the tycoon senate candidate who had done so many wonderful things for low-income housing and his son.

My mind was a chaotic mess, and I knew I wasn't ready to go

to my condo yet. Rather than head home and do one of the many things I needed to, I redirected and drove to the boat. The luxury sailboat had been a bribe from Dad after the divorce, and I loved taking Mom out on it as a giant fuck-you to the old man. That was then. Mom was too sick to handle the waves anymore. Still, it was a good place to think and decompress. I needed to devise a solid plan, and a sunset sail on the lake was where I would do it.

CHAPTER TWO

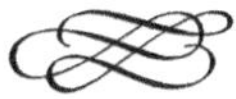

GIA

I slammed into the side of the wall, instantly awake. *Someone's onboard.* A second passed, then two, while I oriented myself, gauging the immediate danger. The boat no longer felt tethered to the dock. The cabin tilted at an angle as the Catalina charged through Lake Michigan's waves. I'd rolled from the center of the bed at the abrupt motion, probably when the sails were hoisted. An uneasy tingling rushed through me and settled uncomfortably in my fingertips. I was well and truly screwed.

My heart thudded loudly in my ears as my body screamed from the potential danger. I'd become good at staying on high alert over the past year, and I wouldn't ignore even the slightest warning—and yet, I had. The luxury cruising sailboat was moving and fast. I'd slept like the dead as the boat had motored out of the harbor and into open waters.

A nap had seemed like a good idea after I'd gone for a run. It hadn't been. I'd lived aboard the forty-three-foot Catalina 425, or the *Quarterback Keeper,* as it was named, for the past week and a half without anyone visiting, and I'd begun to feel safe. *Big fucking mistake.*

I held still, cataloging and dismissing sounds. The door to

the cabin was open, and I heard the snap of sails. *Did I leave it open? Did my ex find me? Is he onboard?* A whimper escaped my lips, and I had to fight through the paralysis of fear before it overcame my ability to do whatever I needed to in the next few moments.

A thump sounded overhead then another. *Footfalls.* I scooted out of bed, dove for the too-small-for-me closet, shoved the clothes aside, and pulled the door shut with a soft click.

I huddled with my knees to my chest, and my mind raced. *Are we far from the docks? Could I jump over the side and swim for shore?* I wasn't a strong swimmer, but I would have a better chance if we were close to land. And it wasn't as though Lake Michigan had sharks.

My brain raced as I plotted my escape. I could get away. I hadn't been discovered. It wasn't him. He never would have let me sleep, not with that giant ego—he would have made sure I knew he'd found me.

If the boat docked, I might be able to slip out unnoticed. New city. New me. I would start again, stay hidden, and keep moving where Dayton wouldn't find me.

I pushed air out of my mouth, slowly and quietly, before dropping my forehead to my raised knees. It'd been so nice living on the boat. I'd felt safe. I couldn't use credit cards, since those could be traced. So, I was left to run and struggle to find a place to sleep every night where I didn't feel like I would be attacked. It was exhausting—which was why I'd lingered on the boat for longer than I should have.

I closed my eyes briefly, surrounded by the scents of laundry detergent and cedar, willing my heart rate to slow. It wasn't the end of the world. I was free, safe, and undiscovered—for the time being.

I shifted then rested my head against the back of the tiny closet and prepared to wait. I couldn't even check my prepaid burner phone to figure out how far we were from the Chicago coast, assuming we were sailing away from and not alongside it. I'd left my phone under the pillow—if it was still there after how the cabin had listed and I'd rolled.

I did some mental calculations and guessed about an hour had passed since I'd gotten back from my run then crashed. *Could we have just left the dock?*

Time passed while I planned how quickly I could grab my meager belongings, shove them into a backpack, and escape without being noticed. I hadn't left things around the boat. They were all in the bedroom, within easy reach of where I'd been squatting.

I'd kept things mostly packed because I knew I might have to dash. But my running shoes and clothes were on the floor. And I'd left a wet towel in the bathroom. If I was lucky, no one would venture down. It would take a miracle for them not to notice my stuff if they did.

The cadence changed. It felt as if we slowed. The cabin seemed to level out, no longer at the angle it had been. *Did we fall off the breeze?* A whirling sound followed, and I imagined the sails automatically rolling down, stowed away as I'd routinely seen them. I jumped at what might be the clink of a chain. We'd dropped anchor. It was quiet except for the slap of water against the boat, which should have been relaxing. To me it wasn't.

I barely breathed, gnawing my lower lip as we drifted within the tether's confines. It would be so much better if whoever was above had only wanted to take the boat out for a short sail and was leaving again. My ears strained to hear the slightest movement. When I wanted to spring from the closet, I forced myself to wait some more. The thought of my ex standing in the primary bedroom, just waiting for me, helped me remain where I was longer.

But it can't be him. I knew it in my heart. Dayton was predictable in some ways. *Letting me sleep in peace?* That wouldn't have happened—not even to get me alone in open water.

A sliver of relief came on the heels of that thought. And when no other sounds came, I wondered if I'd been wrong. Maybe what I'd thought was the anchor had been something else. Possibly the rope scraping against the dock's metal as it was secured. I waited for what seemed like forever before cracking open the closet door. That could be my chance to escape and find a new place to live rent free and undetected.

I threw up a quick prayer to whatever deity was listening, opened the door wide, then tripped over my feet. I landed on my knees just as the bathroom door opened. A naked guy stepped into the bedroom, and I froze against the unmade bed.

The bathroom was in clear sight of where I crouched, pinching my eyes shut. *How could this happen to me?* As he cleared his throat, a deep, masculine rumble echoed through the too-quiet cabin. Slowly, I opened my eyes and followed the trail of naked man from his feet to—*ahh!* I sucked in air like a baby bird waiting for a worm. Um, not the right reference. That was no worm. And he was *not* Dayton.

The dripping-wet man stood with a towel clutched in his hand, frozen as he'd been scrubbing the water from his short, dark hair. I had a bird's-eye view of his impressive package. Or I guess it would be a snake's-eye view.

"See something interesting?" His eyebrow rose.

My throat tightened. Not a sound left me.

"Care to share your thoughts?"

Nope, hard pass on that. He growled. My gaze traveled from his snake—not a worm—to his muscular chest then his bulging biceps. All the while, I worked hard to avoid another peek at his dangly parts. I got tangled in the view of his body. I wasn't afraid of it. I could appreciate the view. What bothered me was being trapped in a small space with someone whose intentions I knew nothing about.

"No." I cleared my throat to bring my voice down from its dog-whistle level to normal. "Nothing to share." I stood on shaky legs, hoping he missed the way my hands trembled. *How can I turn this horrifying situation to my favor?* I scowled, sick of how pretty packages like him had the potential to hide pure ugliness. The fact was, I was trespassing. If I couldn't bluff my way out of my presence there, I might not fare well with whatever he decided to do.

All muscle and a face that would make any girl's head turn—except mine—only drove home how much trouble I was in. A guy with a similar physique and golden-blond good looks had duped me once. I was no fool—not anymore.

"But if I had some clothes, I would definitely offer you some."

He stood there for another minute before grabbing a pair of joggers and pulling them up his long, muscular legs. Of fucking course, they were gray sweats that did nothing to hide the outline of what he was packing. God save me from beautiful men. They weren't worth it—ever.

His face mirrored the scowl I wore. "Who are you, and what are you doing on my boat?"

I mimicked his earlier eyebrow raise and adapted a false bravado. "Your boat? I don't think so. This is my friend's boat. And aren't you a little young to afford something like this?"

He was probably my age, but I tried a guise of confidence and took a chance. It was the sweatpants that made me think he could work for the owner. Lord knew Dayton had people at his beck and call. If the guy only worked on the boat, he could be doing something he wasn't supposed to. Maybe we could come to an arrangement because staying there had allowed me the first good night's sleep since I'd put on my running shoes and gotten the hell out of dodge. I had nowhere to go, no money to get there, and no one to call for help. Dayton had made sure of that.

"What?" The guy's head knocked back, confusion pulling at the corners of his mouth. "Stop fucking around." A mean glint hardened his deep blue eyes. "Are you a reporter?"

"Ah, no." Weird. *Why would he think that?* I was in a T-shirt, sans bra, and a pair of sleep shorts that barely covered my ass. My hair had to look like a squirrel was nesting in it, since I'd crashed after showering and hadn't brushed it out. I gestured to all of me. "Do I look like a reporter?"

I felt how he looked me up and down, a flush spreading over my neck to settle in my cheeks. *Asshole.* I crossed my arms over my chest, hoping to hide the way my nipples saluted him.

"This is private property."

Despite his growly voice, he didn't physically move toward me, luckily, because I couldn't take on his over six feet of height and shoulders like that. But I was so going to jail for trespassing.

A wave of dizziness rolled through me. I blinked, sucked in air, then hardened myself against the flight response that demanded action. "Yeah, I know it's private property, and I'm supposed to be here. What are you doing here? This isn't your boat," I bluffed. That was all the game I had. "And why'd you move it? Are you trying to kidnap me?"

"Listen, lady. I'm losing patience. It's my boat, and I can sail it wherever I want. Which begs the question of who you are." Silence hung expectantly in the air. As the seconds ticked by, he seemed to come to a decision and pulled a phone from his pocket. "I'm calling the cops."

"No." I thrust my hand between us as if I could stop him. The shaking was impossible to hide.

I didn't care. If he called the cops, Dayton would know where I was. He had connections, a friend on the force back in California who probably had my name flagged if it rolled across any police log in the US. He was that kind of connected. There would be no escaping him then. He would make them hold me until he could get to me, and I would never be able to leave again. "Please. No cops."

"Who the fuck let you on my boat?" Though his tone remained commanding, he eased back, lifting his eyes from his phone.

I lowered my arm. The only things between us were the frantic puffs of air leaving my parted lips to crash against his chest.

"It was my dad, wasn't it? Did he set you up here so I would conveniently find you? What's his game now?"

"Your dad?" *What is he talking about?* I dropped onto the bed, my mind whirling with how much trouble I was in. McHottie was probably a spoiled rich kid who snapped his fingers and got whatever he wanted. I snuck a glance at him from under my lashes. I knew people like that—my ex, to be specific. I wasn't liking the comparisons. But something, a strength in the way this guy held himself, didn't telegraph the nastier side of rich and spoiled that I was familiar with.

"Tell me who the fuck you are." His voice cracked through the small space like a whip, authority dripping from each syllable.

My gaze jerked to his at the command, and I responded automatically. "Gia." *How the hell will I get myself out of this mess?* I couldn't try to play him, soften him up. I'd fallen for Mr. Nice on the Eyes before, which was why I was hiding on McHottie's boat. I couldn't do it again.

He grabbed a discarded shirt and pulled it on. Fall Lake University stretched across his impressive chest, and who he was clicked into place.

But how did a college hottie—yeah, I recognized him, because everyone in the football-loving world knew Kylian Wilder was a god—*get a boat as sweet as this one?*

"Did the college buy you the boat?" He was a D1 athlete, and considering how talked about he was, I could see it happening.

A muscle twitched on the side of his chiseled jaw. "My dad did."

Oh shit. My brain finally put two and two together.

His dad was Danbury Wilder, Illinois senatorial candidate. I needed to think fast to make it work in my favor. With his lips still curled back in answer to my question, hatred spilled from Kylian's narrowed gaze.

And isn't that interesting?

CHAPTER THREE

KYLIAN

Gia's pink tongue swiped across her lower lip, and I got hard, which was fucked up, since she looked nervous as hell. And even worse—she could be a plant from my dad. Her eyes kept darting to the exit then back to me. I closed the distance between us as she jumped to her feet, matching each of my steps until her back pressed against the wall. Then I took her place sitting on the bed to hide what was growing in my pants.

I needed to get to the bottom of why she was there. My first instinct that my dad had something to do with it faded based on the fear she was trying to hide. "You need to tell me the truth about why you're on my boat."

"I thought this was my friend's boat."

"You're sticking with that lie?"

The upward tilt of her chin made me want to laugh. Yeah, she was a liar, just maybe not a dangerous one. I had to figure out her angle.

"I tried to call my friend to get the passcode for the door." She flung her arm toward the broken keypad that secured the area. "I'm from out of town, and when Laura didn't answer, I didn't know what else to do."

"Go to a hotel."

She shifted from foot to foot, her eyes darting to the door again. Then her shoulders went back, and her gaze locked and held mine. "Maybe we can make a deal about me staying here."

I took in her long, toned legs and wished I could get a view of her ass. I bet it was spectacular. Without a bra, I could see more than she probably realized through the threadbare pale blue T-shirt. My hand curled by my side as I imagined what her long, wavy dark-brown hair would feel like fisted in it. And her face... She was a showstopper with full pink lips, bright-blue eyes, and high cheekbones. She was attractive—beautiful, actually—but I didn't need anything from her. Better to be blunt about it, especially since she was in the wrong. "I doubt you have anything I need."

"There's got to be something." Straight white teeth sank into her full bottom lip before she released it.

The exchange was entertaining. "What?"

"I could do your homework."

Not what I expected. "I'm on track to graduate magna cum laude. I don't need help with my homework." I let my gaze wander over her body, willing her to offer what I knew she would—what most chicks did so they could make a play to become a future NFL wife.

"Yeah, not that, QB1." She scoffed. "I know your type."

I smirked, loving the back-and-forth. Anything that distracted me from the stress in my life was worth entertaining. "Ah, I see you're an expert in assumptions for people you don't know. Tell me, what type am I?"

"A notorious womanizer who apparently has more money than sense."

I laughed because she had that wrong in so many ways. "Notorious, huh?" I shook my head, ready to be done with the discussion. I'd had a hell of a week. All I'd wanted to do was take the boat out to relieve some stress and find some much-needed peace. And with her there, that wasn't happening. I needed to get back and sleep, not spar with the stowaway. I had class in the morning, football practice in the afternoon, weights, watching film, then homework. "Look, this has been entertaining, but the fact is you're trespassing, and you can't offer anything to strike a deal."

"Yeah, I meant what I said, and you must need help with something, especially after the loss against Michigan. That was quite a game." She planted a fist on her hip, fire dancing in her eyes. "Three interceptions last Saturday, a fumble, and four sacks because you're too comfy in the pocket. Too slow to protect yourself when the line breaks down."

Huh, she could talk football and had watched that shit show. It'd been slippery as hell from slanting rain and punishing wind that day. Mom had had her first experimental treatment, and my head had not been where it should've been. On top of that, my offense hadn't been stopping the defense's left tackle from breaking the line. That fucker was quick.

"That was last week. Catch this Saturday's game?" I knocked my head in the TV's direction. "On my TV?"

She pursed her lips, and I snorted a laugh.

"I appreciate the fandom, whether I shit the bed that week or not, but this is my boat, and why the fuck are you really here? Truth time, or I'm calling the cops, which I should have done when I first came aboard."

Her eyes went wide. "No fucking cops."

"Then tell me the truth and not this bullshit about a made-up friend."

"Fine," she gritted between clenched teeth. "I needed a place to stay, and the boat was empty."

"You knew it was my boat and thought you could take advantage."

"Of what?" Her voice rose to a higher octave, pink staining her cheeks.

"The way you popped out of the closet when I came out of the shower was too convenient. It reeks of a setup."

"You're crazy." Long fingers thrust into her hair, and she tilted her head back, which pushed her breasts against her T-shirt.

There was no way the girl wasn't playing me with that move. Cold, calculating fury hardened me to her game.

She dropped her hands and glared at me with pure hatred. "Trust me. You don't have anything I want or need."

"Except my boat."

More color leached from her face, taking some of my anger with it. Maybe I was a fool, but I was starting to believe she really needed a place to stay. *Could it be she hadn't singled me out? Or am I just a sucker? Easily conned and probably by my dad?* He'd certainly taken me for a fool when I was young, and he'd taught me to sail while on his visitation time. It hadn't been for me at all. It was so his buddies would see, and if someone happened to write an article on the business tycoon spending time with his son, all the better. I shook off the memories. They had no place in my head.

Still, I thought back to when she'd popped out of the closet and the surprise and fear on her face when she saw me. It was later, when I put on a Fall Lake University shirt, that recognition sparked in her eyes as to who I was. It was a long shot, backed only by the lack of family pictures or identifying information she could have seen on the boat.

Distrust crackled between us. If, and that was a big if, she had no connection to my pops or the media, she might be able to do something for me. I clinically scanned her fuck-hot body and gorgeous face. It could work, and after dinner with Mom, I felt helpless—a particular feeling I despised. So, I took a chance. "We can work something out, since I have what you need."

Her gaze dropped to where my dick strained toward her. Even sitting on the bed couldn't quite hide it. "Gross. No. I'm not sucking your dick so I can stay here."

"I don't need to pay to get that," I snapped. Fuck, she pissed me the hell off. I took a breath, needing to keep my head because I had a feeling we could use each other in a mutually beneficial way. She was scared. Didn't have somewhere to live. I could use those things to help both of us. "You need a place to crash, right?"

She crossed her arms over her chest and shifted on her feet. "Yes."

The barely concealed terror swimming through her blue eyes convinced me she was telling enough of the truth to go ahead and negotiate a deal. "I have an idea for an arrangement that would let you stay here rent-free."

CHAPTER FOUR

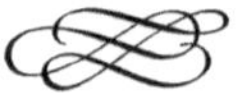

GIA

Rent-free? I wanted to jump on his offer, to just say yes. Good thing I wasn't as naïve as I used to be. He was a man. A stranger. I couldn't trust him. I'd learned that lesson far too well.

He hadn't moved from the bed, but I didn't buy the way he'd done that to appear less intimidating. I knew his impressive stats—and that ESPN loved every inch of his six-foot-three and hundred eighty-five pounds of pure muscle. According to them, so would the upcoming draft. Kylian Wilder was going places. None that included me. *So, where do I fit in?*

"What's the catch?" I couldn't help it. I bit—out of stupid curiosity and, the real driving factor, pure desperation.

"I have a few questions before I explain my proposition." He leaned forward, elbows on his knees.

The movement put him closer. My stupid heart rate kicked into a gallop, and I fought the urge to retreat a step. He took up too much damn space as it was. A weird energy crackled between us—nothing I wanted to look into. He was a reminder of temptation that I wouldn't give into. I couldn't afford to fall from such heights again.

"Is there a warrant out for your arrest?"

Fair question. "No."

"How old are you?"

"I'm not underage." *Where is he going with this?*

"You look young. I'm not sure I believe you. I'll want to see a driver's license." He scanned my body. "For now, tell me your age."

Fine. "Twenty-one."

"What's your full legal name?"

"Why?" I wasn't comfortable with that territory. "What will you do if I tell you?"

"If you aren't wanted by the police, it's a fair question."

Maybe. *Can I trust him?* As badly as things could have gone with him finding me, nothing had happened. And I didn't sense malicious vibes. His confidence and authority—not the bad kind that I was used to—eased some of my fear. I opened my mouth to tell him. Nothing came out. I couldn't do it. "Tell me why first. I don't know you, and I have no reason to trust you."

He studied me, and a shiver raced through my already-alert body. He looked at me as if he could see all my carefully guarded secrets, and I didn't want him inside.

"I want you to pretend to be my girlfriend then my wife."

"What?" That came out a little louder than I'd expected. Still... "Your wife?" A bitter laugh fell from my lips. "QB1, you're out of your ever-lovin' mind if you think I'll pretend to be your wife." I stepped forward then caught myself. He was crazy, and I needed to keep my wits about me—and distance between us.

"Let me clarify." He straightened, pushing his elbows off his knees, but stayed seated. "I don't want you to pretend. I want to present you to my mom as my girlfriend, then I'll fake propose. We'll get married and stay together for as long as my mom lives."

I snapped my mouth closed. I hadn't realized it was hanging open. "What's wrong with you?" *For real, though, what's wrong with him that he would need me—a stranger—to marry him?* "The answer is no."

"We can help each other." He paused, and something warred through his eyes before he seemed to reach a decision. "My mom is sick, and I don't know how long she has left. Her biggest wish is to see me married. It'll take me years to find someone else, date, and marry them. I don't have that kind of time."

"I'm sorry about your mom, but that's not my problem."

"No, it isn't. But a place to stay is. And maybe money too?"

I felt the sucker punch as if it were real. He had my number, but I wasn't the only one with an ace up my sleeve—he needed me just as badly. "Why me? Don't you have any female friends who can do this? Aren't there thousands of jersey chasers who'll happily be Mrs. Saturday Afternoon Quarterback Keeper?"

"Yeah, there are."

He smirked, making me frown. *Cocky much?*

"But they'll want it to be real. This, between us, is a business arrangement. I need someone who is no-nonsense and understands that a deal is a deal."

That, I could get behind. "What do I get out of this arrangement? A place to live, obviously, but what else?" If I could get more out of him, I was not above exploiting him for it. He owned the boat, even if his daddy bought it for him. I bet he had access to lots of money. I'd blown through what little I'd managed to take with me, and I could use some in case I had to make another quick exit.

"I'll pay you to do whatever I need"—he rolled his eyes at my narrowed gaze—"not sexual, and we'll split amicably when it's over."

"And when will that be?"

That muscle along his jaw ticked, and... *Are his eyes getting red?*

"When my mom dies."

My heart lurched as his words pierced my mind. Grief broke

as clear as day on his face. The wall barricading his emotions dropped, giving me a breath-stealing glimpse into his pain. For our negotiation, he let me see it all, and God, I felt for him. I was no stranger to death and loss.

"I hate to ask this"—my stomach churned and rebelled—"but in reference to the business deal, how long does she have?"

"Months." He cleared his throat then scrubbed his hands over his face. "It could be one month or six."

I blinked back tears for a woman I didn't even know. Getting ahold of my emotions, I turned the conversation back to business. "What are the terms with living arrangements? If this is your daddy's boat, won't he take offense to me staying on it?" Because I had a suspicion that even if it was a gift from his dad, it could be snatched back.

"If that becomes a problem, you'll move in with me."

"And where do you live? Do you have roommates?"

"I live in a three-bedroom condo. There's a doorman, and I have two roommates."

"Both footballers?"

At his nod, my mind spun. More muscle. More safety. It might help keep Dayton at bay once he found out where I was— and he would. Because he was relentless when he wanted something, and he thought of me as his—bought and paid for.

"Well?"

"I just… Give me a minute." I paced along the edge of the bed in front of him. The money would be nice. And the security. If he followed through with the deal, it would be a fair one for both of us, one he couldn't go back on because I could take it public or sue. And I bet his father wouldn't want that kind of publicity. I stopped in front of him, my decision made. "Fine. Let's negotiate."

A slow grin curved his firm lips, and all I could think about was how they would feel, which was all kinds of wrong. I told myself I didn't want him—or any man, for that matter—

touching me. When he stood, towering over me, my pulse spiked for reasons I didn't want to identify. He came back to the bed with a notebook and pen. I sat across from him.

An hour later, notes scribbled over several pages defined the finer points of our agreement.

"I'm not having sex with you."

"I didn't say anything about sex, Gia. However, we have to look like we're intimate when we're out in public or around my parents."

"What exactly do you mean? Hand-holding?" *Please let it just be that.*

"Yes, and kissing in public."

"I don't like it."

"It's nonnegotiable."

I could see his point, but I wished it weren't necessary. For the added security, to be safe, I would deal with it. "Fine. What else?"

"Dinner once a week with my mom."

That didn't feel right. "Twice a week, since this is all for your mom anyway."

He studied me in that too-close way he had. "Do you have family?"

"No."

He put down the pen. "Are you enrolled in college? It might be easier to transfer you to Fall Lake University."

"I was in college somewhere else. I don't want to enroll again."

"You can stay on the boat unless something happens and you don't feel safe."

"What do you mean?" *Could he know? Does he know Dayton? Is this a setup?*

"The lock is broken."

"Oh." Air whooshed from my lungs. "Yeah, I'm okay. You're the only one who's come on board since I started staying here."

"How long has that been?"

"Just under two weeks."

He took it in stride, and I was able to breathe easy.

"You might need to move in with me when we're engaged. It depends on how things pan out with my dad being my dad."

"What does that even mean?"

"The less time you spend alone with him, the better."

Yeah, we would have to circle back around to that eventually. "If I have to move into your place, I'm not cooking for you. Or cleaning up after you. Or doing your laundry."

"I'm capable of doing all that myself. As for cleaning, I have a housekeeper who comes in once a week."

"Just shows that I was right with my first assessment."

He locked gazes with me, and I felt the heat like the three feet between us didn't exist. I leaned back an inch. Didn't matter. I planned to keep him on his toes and physically as far away from me as possible.

"Spoiled rich kid."

The air felt charged, but he didn't rise to my bait. "My lawyer will draw up the contract with the terms we've agreed to here. There'll be a prenup and a payout guarantee once the divorce is final."

"And how much will that be?"

"Fifty grand."

That could get me out of the country and living somewhere Dayton's reach didn't extend. "If you're using a lawyer, I'm guessing he's from dear old Dad. How do you expect to keep our arrangement a secret?"

"My lawyer isn't associated with my dad. No one will ever know, so long as you do your part, sign the NDA, and don't speak about our agreement."

I nodded, exhaustion washing over me despite the short nap I'd taken earlier. It was the adrenaline from getting caught. It'd drained what little energy I'd managed to recoup. "Is there anything else?"

"If there is, we'll amend the original contract. Add your signature on this one to keep the details between us. My lawyer will have everything prepared and ready to sign by tomorrow night. I'll come find you when I have it."

My heart thudded loudly in my ears, a fast-paced clock ticking down to a decision I couldn't make lightly. If I went forward with our deal, I would be locked in. I pinched the pen tightly between my fingers, hesitating as I weighed my options. I didn't have many, and what he proposed wasn't to be taken lightly.

I dropped the pen like it was hot. "I need more time to think about this."

Several seconds passed before he responded, adding to the frantic pounding of my pulse.

"Okay, I get it. Sleep on it." He tapped the papers then stood and moved toward the door leading to the upper deck. "I'll be back at six in the morning. I'll need your decision then."

T he evening crawled as I waffled over what I should do—sign the document or run. The last thing I wanted was to put anyone at risk. Because if my asshole ex, Dayton, found out anyone was helping me, coming between him and who he thought belonged to him, there would be hell to pay—for all parties involved.

I flopped onto my stomach, glad the boat was docked once again. It was truly the safest place for me to stay. Dayton wouldn't go anywhere near water—his one true kryptonite, since he couldn't swim. That alone had almost been reason enough for me to sign Kylian's terms.

Throughout the night and into the early-morning hours, I

stalked Dayton online to ensure he wasn't in pursuit. I liked knowing he was back where he belonged, which was far from me.

It wasn't until three in the morning that I came across the article about a huge gala and noticed one photograph in particular. My hands shook as I held my phone, studying Dayton's arm around Cynthia—the woman who used to chase him shamelessly whenever we ran into her at the society events like the one they were at.

Could he have moved on?

It took reading the article three times to find the small notice about Cynthia Thompson attending a high-society gala with my ex. We had been together for a year, and for the past six months, I'd been on the run. *Could it finally be over?*

Even if it was—and I wasn't positive he would give up that easily—I wouldn't push my luck and wave a flag with my location on it or drop my guard completely. It would be safer to stay on the water and stick with Kylian's added muscle and notoriety.

The papers Kylian had written our mutual terms on were within arm's reach. He was due to arrive in a mere two hours, but I didn't have to wait. Not any longer. After pulling them into my lap along with the pen, I signed, giving up my last name on paper. We had a deal.

CHAPTER FIVE

KYLIAN

Several days had passed, and the ink from Gia's signature and mine was dry on the contract my lawyer had sent over. The argument we'd had several days ago, about who she was and why she was on my boat, was mostly forgotten.

It was a goddamned miracle she let me drive her to my mom's place. That'd been an hour-long argument I couldn't get back. *Had I known she was so stubborn, or cautious about being alone with me in my SUV, would I still have gone through with it?* I glanced at the leggy brunette sitting next to me in a pretty blue-and-white sundress that fell to midthigh. Yep. I would. A hundred percent yes. She was hot as fuck, and when she pushed my buttons, she made me forget how sad I was.

I turned down Mom's street then pulled up along the curb not far from the run-down brownstone. I put the SUV in park and took a deep breath. That was it. We needed a game plan, and the best way to execute it was to share information. "I need to prepare you before we go inside."

Gia and I sat in silence while I struggled with what to say.

The idea that Mom wouldn't be there at some point—and watching her fade away—killed me. "Mom has a hard time accepting help, but she needs it. The treatments take a lot out of her."

The tension between us eased a little, and I was grateful that she let me take the time to think about what I wanted to share with her.

"Mom is the most important person in my life. She's been my biggest cheerleader, no matter what shit we went through." I let the reality of our well-intentioned deceit settle over me. It was the right thing to do. Anything was if it brought her joy. "It's my turn to be hers."

Gia gave my hand a brief squeeze, then she quickly retreated to her side. The rare show of solidarity between us was enough.

I got out of the SUV, and it was blissfully silent as we climbed the stairs to my mom's apartment, while I fought the strange urge to grab Gia's hand. I ran my palms down the sides of my jeans before knocking on the door.

"Relax, superstar," Gia whispered. "This'll be a piece of cake."

I grinned but noticed how she'd tucked her hair behind her ears more than once. She was just as nervous as I was. I guessed that was good. At least she was taking it seriously. It'd been four days since we'd signed the contract. I'd also fixed the keypad she'd broken on the boat and told her the passcode. We'd exchanged numbers, too, and I'd given her some spending money. It wasn't much, just a couple hundred dollars to get her through the upcoming weeks.

"Hey, don't call me superstar around my mom. My dad does that, and she hates it." I did, too, but the only information that mattered was about Mom.

Gia observed me with wide eyes. "Is your dad here too?"

In this dump? He might have owned it and been one of the acting slumlords, but he wouldn't be caught dead in there. "No. They're divorced."

"Okay."

"You don't follow politics?" I could have sworn she knew

who my dad was, that there was recognition of more than my football status as Fall Lake's starting quarterback.

"Not that well. I do when it's time to know the issues so I can make a well-informed vote."

I placed my hand on her lower back and got a glare that made me laugh. "You'll have to get used to me touching you."

"Not when no one is around." She sidestepped, adding distance between us and effectively shrugging off my hand.

A part of me wondered why she was going along with the deal. *Is it just about the money and a place to stay? Or is there another reason?* The questions swam in my mind as we waited for Mom to answer. I would bet all my money—what little was left, sixty thousand to be exact—that there was more to Gia's story.

The door opened, and I had less than a second to school my features. But fuck—Mom looked like she'd lost even more weight from the nothing that she had to spare. Her cheeks were gaunt, her collarbones more pronounced.

"Welcome!"

Mom wrapped her too-thin arms around me, and I pretended for that one second that she wasn't smaller and weaker and that I wasn't worried about snapping her in half if I hugged her too hard. She turned to Gia and hugged her before waving us into the apartment.

"It's so nice to meet you, Gia." Mom shot a reproachful glance my way. "Kylian's been keeping you a secret, but I'm glad I have the chance to get to know you now."

"I am too." Gia smiled.

"What'd you make? It smells amazing."

My stomach growled in approval, and Mom laughed.

"Stuffed pork chops." Each step toward the kitchen was slow.

I wrapped my arm around her waist to help, but she swatted my hand away.

"I'm fine, Kyl. Stop hovering."

"Mrs. Wilder, can I do anything? Set the table?"

"Call me Evalyn. And everything's set, except for pulling the pork chops out of the oven and getting the rolls from the toaster. I had all day to get ready for you two to visit. Kyl, why don't you shut the TV off, and Gia and I can put the food on the table?"

I left them alone for as long as it took to do as Mom had asked. The living room appeared as if she'd vacuumed. *Maybe?* It was hard to tell, since the carpet didn't fluff up anymore. Everything else was in its original place. Only her blanket sat askew on the recliner, with her tea on the end table. The place was still depressing. Anger for how Mom lived rolled through me, and I had to take a second to breathe. She would notice and chastise me about how she liked her place. Her friends were there. I'd heard it all before, and it wasn't the best time to rehash it.

I paused at the entry to the kitchen, watching the two women interact.

Gia leaned forward and inhaled while carrying the dish. "Did you use apple in your stuffing?"

Mom beamed as Gia set the heavy dish on the small kitchen table. "Yes. It adds nice flavor and helps the pork chops stay moist. Not many people know that."

As I slipped into the kitchen, I caught the renewed interest in Mom's expression as she eyed Gia.

"Sit." Mom waved us to our seats. "I wanted to do something special, since it's our first evening together, and this used to be one of Kyl's favorite meals."

"Anything you cook is my favorite." I kissed her on the cheek before pulling out her chair. I rubbed a hand over my chest, massaging the slight ache from watching Gia be kind to Mom.

Mom smoothed her napkin over her lap with trembling fingers. Before she tried to lift anything, I served her then passed the food to Gia. She'd overextended herself, and I was annoyed that I hadn't insisted on bringing takeout. Seeing her so fragile and tired scared the hell out of me. Mom was my rock, and I didn't know what I would do without her. First Grandad had passed, then Dad had changed and eventually divorced Mom, and after I started college, she'd been diagnosed with cancer. I was fucking terrified of losing her. It'd been us against the world for so long.

"Tell me about yourself." Mom didn't bother eating as she focused her attention on Gia.

"I'm not that interesting." Gia set her fork on her plate and smiled. "I moved here not too long ago from California, where I was living with Uncle Jimmy. After he died, I realized I needed a change of scenery. And here I am."

California? I should have been asking her questions instead of prepping her for dinner. I leaned back in my chair, chewing slowly. *But would it have made a difference?* With me, she was tight-lipped. One conversation with my mom, and she willingly opened up. *Or was her story a lie?* I wouldn't put it past her.

"And here you are." Mom beamed, erasing the lines of tension that'd bracketed her mouth for so many months. "I'm sorry to hear about your uncle. Do you have relatives living nearby?"

"No." Gia tucked her hair behind her ear again. "It was always me and Mom. My dad was never in the picture. She caught an antibiotic-resistant pneumonia when I was just going into middle school and passed away suddenly. My uncle, her brother, took me in."

"I'm so sorry." Mom reached across the table and covered Gia's hand, which she gave a light squeeze before letting go. "Such a hard time too."

I found myself drawn into Gia's orbit, barely resisting the urge to put my arm around her shoulders and pull her close. But a gesture like that so early in our newfound alliance would make her uncomfortable, and I didn't want Mom to witness her pulling away from me.

"Yeah." Gia shrugged, a rueful grin curving her pink lips. "I wasn't that easy to get along with at first. That's when Uncle Jimmy introduced me to football and cooking. Once we established a routine, living without Mom slowly became bearable, and I came to love staying with my uncle."

"Well, I can see how your love of football makes things easier for Kylian. It takes up a lot of his time, and if he goes into the NFL like he plans, it'll be even more demanding."

"We'll make it work." Gia's smile was sweet and sincere.

"Though"—Mom shot me a piercing glance—"NFL careers aren't always long. Just make sure you two are in this relationship for the right reasons."

Nice, that was a not-so-subtle warning to make sure Gia wasn't after me for money.

Laughter spilled from Gia, lightening the mood and easing the tension in Mom's shoulders. "Oh, trust me, we are. I didn't even know who your son was the first time we met. He made a big impression, an impossible one to walk away from."

I choked on my water, the way we met a clear visual in my mind. "This is amazing, Mom." I changed the subject. "But you didn't have to go to all this trouble. Gia and I want to come over again in a few days, and we'll bring food. Whatever you want."

"Nonsense." She picked up her fork, cut a few pieces of pork chop, and moved food around her plate. "You need a good home-cooked meal."

"I love to cook." Gia took a sip of water. "My uncle was a Michelin chef. He taught me everything I know, and I would be happy to come over and either help or make dinner for you."

"Impressive. And thank you, I would love that." Mom took a small bite. "When did you two meet?"

All my alarms blared at full blast. *How could we have forgotten to cover that?* My mind raced to come up with a plausible story. At the slight pause, Mom's hand froze, her food halfway to her mouth, and her eyes narrowed on us. I didn't want her to jump to conclusions because she had never liked anyone I'd dated in the past. No one was good enough, or they were using me. It was always something. She wasn't wrong, but I was using them, too, never wanting anything serious out of our arrangements. Mom just refused to see that part.

Gia's eyes were wide, a hint of panic constricting her pupils.

I took point on the question. "We met a couple of months ago at a party. We've been seeing each other every chance we can. I would have brought her around to meet you sooner, but it's been busy with school and football."

"Will you excuse me for a minute?"

Gia mouthed *bathroom* to me while Mom scrutinized my response.

I pointed her in the right direction, waiting until she left and the door shut before I turned back to Mom. "What's going on? Don't you like her?"

"The girl is wonderful, Kylian, but there's no sign that you two even like each other."

"What are you talking about? Of course we do." Sweat beaded along my spine. Mom was like a dog with a bone if she sensed something amiss. *What did we do—other than forgetting to script how we met—to screw this up?*

"You don't touch. You barely look at each other."

My hand curled into a fist beneath the table, and it struck me like a lightning bolt how much I'd wanted to touch Gia. "We're just nervous because this is so important to us both."

"Please." Mom huffed. "When have you ever cared if I liked your girlfriends before?"

Leaning across the table, I had the perfect response. "When have I brought one around to meet you? Not since high school, and Tiffany doesn't count because that relationship crashed and burned after she found out I was going to college here after she got into Notre Dame."

We both fell silent as Gia returned, her expression wary as she read the room. "Is everything okay?"

"We were just talking, and I wondered how you managed to outfox all the photographers following Kylian since they named him one of Chicago's most eligible bachelors."

"Oh, that." Gia laughed, and I hoped Mom didn't see how panicky she looked. "It hasn't been much of an issue."

"Obviously, since there hasn't been a single picture in any paper of you together."

"Mom, stop giving her the third degree. Gia's a master of disguise. Plus, we've been meeting up where the reporters haven't followed me."

"Yep. His boat." Gia winked.

"So she's escaped a lot of the media hype," I added.

"I didn't want my picture in any of the papers." Gia rested her elbows on the table and steepled her fingers. "We didn't know where things were going before, so staying off the media's radar made sense. But with how close we've gotten lately…"

"Which is why I wanted to bring her here to meet you. Things are serious." I threaded my fingers with Gia's, ignoring how tightly she squeezed my hand. "She's the one, Mom, and it's important to me that you meet her. That the two of you get along."

Mom made a noncommittal sound then changed the subject. After we cleared the plates, had dessert, and Mom looked like she was about to pass out, we left.

Despite her glare at the subtle touch, I gently nudged Gia out the door and down the stairs until we got into the SUV. "This isn't working. She's not buying that we're into each other. We need to make an addendum to our original deal."

CHAPTER SIX

GIA

Kylian's words to his mom about me being "the one" hadn't been real. My fingers shook as I clicked my seat belt into place. Light shone through the windows from the streetlights' soft glow, which illuminated rows of parked cars along the street. As we left his mom's place after dinner, Kylian seemed to be in a mood. I was conflicted and, as he pulled away from the curb, taking turns faster than I was comfortable with, agitated.

The stereo's bass reverberated through the back of my seat and into my chest. "Where are we going?" My hands curled around the door handle as Kylian wove in and out of traffic, making me nervous as his foot pressed the gas harder. As I tracked the street names and landmarks, I realized we weren't driving to the marina. "Hey!" My voice pierced through the loud music as I pressed my body against the door. My heart pounded in my chest, but I refused to paint Kylian in the same light as my ex. He hadn't done anything, and I was stronger than that. "I *asked you a question.*"

"Relax. We're going to my place to talk."

"Are you for real? *Relax?* Did you want to get into a fight?"

Idiot. I embraced anger over fear. *Because really... telling me to relax?* And I was ignoring how I'd told him the same thing when we stood in front of his mom's apartment door. Totally different. "This could be our first argument as a fake couple."

We stopped at a light, and he rubbed his eyes with his fingers, his weariness tangible. "Wrong word choice. I thought it would be good for you to see where I lived and maybe meet my roommates so you're not blindsided by questions in the future."

The brewing urge to fight with Kylian left me. I eased back in my seat, uncurling stiff fingers from the door handle. "Fine." I couldn't lie. I was a little curious about where Mr. Hotshot Football Star lived—mainly because I loved watching the sport. I had fond memories of watching weekend games on the TV and a feast I cooked with my uncle for every single one. When Dayton came around, he barely contained his disdain for football. I'd given up too much for Dayton—the tradition of food and football I'd had with my uncle was one thing among many.

We drove in silence until we pulled into an underground parking lot beneath a beautiful, nine-story building. I took note of the doorman. *And were those reporters?* I quickly turned my head away and raised my hand to block their view, worried they'd taken a picture of us as we'd pulled in. A camera had been angled toward the SUV, and a flash had gone off. Kylian parked, and I shoved the worry away. I was probably mistaken and overly paranoid.

As I got out of his SUV, his hand rested on the small of my back, and the same jolt of unwanted electricity from the last time he'd touched me shot through my body. I eased away and, instead, latched onto the annoyance from tilting my head so much just to glare at him. "No one's here. You don't get to touch me when it's not for show."

It wasn't being touched that bothered me. It was how it happened. I wasn't scared of men, or sex, but I was terrified of violence. I'd had enough time to lessen my reactions around people unless someone moved fast and in just the right way. It was a trigger, one I hoped I would heal from and escape.

"If my touch makes you pull away, then we need to do it more. It's not a big deal."

It was a big deal. I was too aware of him. I didn't want to feel any sort of attraction. And how my body reacted to his—that alone was dangerous because my mind wasn't ready. I didn't trust him, not yet.

"These little things make us look comfortable together. Right now, we aren't, so I'll keep doing things like that or holding your hand. And before you try to deny it, my mom picked up on it."

He stabbed at the elevator button, then his hand brushed against my back again. A shiver climbed my spine, and I bit my lip to stop from telling him to back off. His hand fell away as we stepped inside and turned to face the doors that closed with a quiet whoosh. He was on the top floor and had to use some card in front of the scanner to propel the elevator into motion.

Why am I not surprised by all this?

Dayton had money. Loads of it. More than he knew what to do with, and he threw it around to control situations that didn't go his way—including me. Trust-fund kids. *What's that life even like?* I had a taste of it with him until he soured my palate with his controlling ways. I'd lost too much of myself just to please him. Nothing was worth putting up with how he'd treated me. Making a run for it was the best decision I'd made from the moment I'd agreed to go on a date with him, a few months after my uncle had passed away.

I shook my head, dislodging the memories, and focused on what Kylian would show me instead. The doors opened to a hallway with only two doors on either end. We went left, and after he opened it, we stepped into a small foyer that led into the living room. From their spots on the couch, two huge guys played a video game on a large TV.

One glanced in our direction, his eyes widening when they landed on me. "Hey, Kyl. How's your mom doing?"

"Tired but good."

He grabbed my hand, and I let him lead me into the living room. A gorgeous kitchen sat to our right, and I got caught up in the Viking appliances and quartz countertops. I wanted to cook in there so badly. It'd been too long, and the boat didn't count with its smaller galley and sparce pots and pans.

I stumbled, and his hand tightened around mine. Heat climbed my cheeks, and I ignored the kitchen, paying attention to where we were going. We stopped to the side of where his roommates sat.

"Gia, this is Ares and Liam," Kylian introduced us after they paused the game.

"Hi." I took in their wide shoulders and athletic builds. Their smiles were friendly, and I sensed nothing malicious behind their relaxed mannerisms.

"Nice to meet you." The one I thought was Ares was the bigger of the two and wore a faded gray-and-blue Fall Lake football T-shirt.

The tension between my shoulder blades eased. He had a chill vibe for the most part. And bonus, he kept his kind topaz eyes on my face. I liked him immediately.

"Hey." Liam's voice was smooth and deep as his green eyes traveled from the top of my head to my toes then back up again. A slow, sexy smile curved his chiseled face. He, too, was gorgeous. And the scar on his cheekbone only enhanced his appeal—not to me, of course. But I imagined women in general would find him irresistible.

Heartbreaker. I pegged him as a womanizer. *But maybe a harmless one?* My instincts didn't scream at me to make a run for it.

"We ordered out," Ares said. "Leftovers are in the fridge if you guys are still hungry. But I imagine not after Evalyn cooked dinner. Man, I miss going with you."

"Thanks, but we're good." Kylian nudged me toward one of the doors. "We've got a few things to talk about."

"I bet you do," Liam said quietly, but the sound traveled.

Kylian shut the door behind us. "Ignore them."

"Planned on it." I crossed my arms over my chest and took in his room. It was larger than I expected. I could see a little of the en suite bathroom but not enough. I wanted to explore everything. The room had white walls and dark-gray accents from the bedspread. A desk, computer, and dresser made up the rest of the furniture. It was surprisingly clean and didn't smell like a sweaty guy, which shocked me. *Aren't all college athletes slobs?* In my limited experience, they were.

I eyed the choices warily, crossed the room to the desk chair, and sat.

He took the bed. His eyes crinkled at the corners, and his lips twitched.

I wasn't there for his amusement. It was time I reminded him. "Let's get this over with. I want to get out of here."

"Lots to do tonight?"

I frowned, not liking his tone. "Yep. You're not my keeper." Because he needed me to give his mother her wish, I was his, though. It made me want to laugh until the weight of my situation crashed back into my thoughts. He sort of had the upper hand, and I didn't like it. Nor would I let him think that. "You're the one who needs my help. So, what do you want to talk about?"

He leaned over the bedside table and withdrew a small black box. When he opened it and took out a ring, I froze.

"Here." Gently, he took my left hand and slid the large solitaire emerald cut diamond set in a white gold band on my finger. I was too shocked to do or say anything.

"We need to publicly announce our engagement to show my parents we're serious."

"Wait." I leaned back, words filling my head once more. "There's no reason to go to extremes. We told your mom. We'll keep playing that game. She'll buy into it." I purposely ignored the heavy weight on my hand. "And what's this parents thing? We only talked about convincing your mom we were serious."

"My dad is a problem that needs to be contained. My mom is skeptical, and our deal was to ensure she's happy and secure that my future is what she's hoping it'll be. She wants to see me happy." He gestured to the ring. "That'll help. Please wear it."

Tension rolled off him in waves. He looked miserable, and I got it after meeting his mom and seeing how close they were. She was dying. It was her last wish, and he wanted to do whatever he could to give it to her, even if it wasn't real. And that was the kicker—I had to help sell it so she would have peace. That meant the ring stayed. I didn't like it, but I would deal.

I wasn't immune to his plight. I wished I'd had more time with my mom, with my uncle. Kylian's time with his mom was finite, and what she wanted wasn't a bad thing. Even the game he and I were playing was out of love.

"Look, I get it. And I'll do my part by allowing a bare minimum of touching to convince her we're the real deal. But that's it. Flag on the play, QB1. We aren't announcing our engagement publicly."

"We have to." Elbows on his knees, he ran his fingers through his hair, looking all kinds of tortured. "My mom wasn't exaggerating. Ever since that stupid fucking hundred-most-eligible-bachelors article came out, I'm newsworthy. We can't avoid the reporters. It'll get out. Better that we control the press than it controls us."

"You posed for that picture in the magazine. It isn't like you've exactly shied away from it. But I don't have to be a part of the publicity drive." *And I won't let him risk my safety and peace of mind so he can stay in the spotlight.*

"I'll give you ten thousand more to announce our engagement publicly."

"No." I would rather die than put a picture in the paper or online, which would lead Dayton right to my doorstep—or Kylian's doorstep, as it were. I came to Chicago to hide. To get lost in the chaos of the population, to be invisible. I couldn't do a widely viewed photo shoot with him, and since he was pretty much a guaranteed first-round draft pick, it would be national news. "No fucking way."

"Fine. Twenty thousand."

"Nope." I didn't even twitch. *But he did, right around his sexy—I mean stubborn—mouth.*

He narrowed his eyes. "Thirty."

Something slammed, or dropped, outside of Kylian's room, and I started, my body trembling. I took a deep breath, willing myself to regain control, doing my best to ignore Kylian's narrowed eyes. Yeah, he caught my reaction. It wouldn't take long for him to realize I wasn't quite right. Pushing that worry away, I dealt with the more pressing one as I tried to hide my internal response.

I looked at my nails, desperately trying to ignore the icky feeling of panic crawling up my spine from the loud noise and, even worse, from him using money to get me to do something. "Not happening."

He stood, seething, fists clenched by his sides. "Why the fuck not?"

"Oh, hell no." I motioned between us. I didn't like how he'd moved or the frustration that pinched his lips. "We're not doing this."

"Fifty K."

I launched myself out of the chair, anxious about the way he was tossing money around—*just like Dayton*—and carefully skirted around him. Then I stormed out of his condo. My finger punched the elevator button repeatedly as I cursed about not knowing where the stairs were. I could feel him approaching behind me, but I heard one of his roommates get up, stop him, and ask what was happening. It endeared me to the roommate in ways he would never know because I wouldn't tell him. But I needed someone on my side, and in that moment, he was—I was pretty sure it was Ares.

The elevator doors opened, and I hit the close button until they slid shut. Kylian's heated gaze burned into me the entire time. A cold sweat covered my forehead, and I wiped it away with shaky fingers as I sagged against the back wall. Kylian hadn't made me nervous. It was the thought of the press taking my picture. Dayton would find me, and no level of security on that boat would keep me safe. I'd already broken in once. I wasn't confident his fear of water would stop him from coming for me if he found out I was dating someone else. And when he found me...

On the sidewalk, beneath a streetlamp, my vision tunneled. The blackness grew in my peripheral vision, and my airway restricted as my breath sawed in and out. I'd had enough panic attacks toward the end of my time with Dayton to recognize what it was. My thoughts spun, and with frantic, jerky movements, I spied a diner ahead.

Keep going. I had to make it to a booth, fall into it, and order a coffee. They would leave me alone for a while. I could get myself under control then.

Where will I go if the option to stay on the boat is gone? I had a crap phone and only a small bag with the few things I'd managed to grab while escaping Dayton.

Time crawled and sped forward weirdly as I pushed through the diner's entrance. Once in a booth, I ordered coffee then sat with my hands curled around the mug, absorbing the warmth. It was September and not as hot as it had been earlier in the evening. Still, I was freezing. I counted each breath, focusing on slowing it down.

Then, when I felt like I could draw in air without hyperventilating, I counted five things I could see, touch, smell, and taste. The condiments in the metal container at the edge of my table—ketchup, mustard, salt, pepper, and a smaller container with jams and sugars. Silverware clinked against plates while people ate. Conversation buzzed around me. The waitress's shoes squeaked. The noises helped ground me. The bell jingled as someone left or entered. The mug felt warm and comforting in my hands, and the bitter taste of the coffee hit my tongue as I sipped the hot liquid.

I didn't know how long I sat there, but with each minute that ticked by, the world around me settled as I convinced myself I was safe. Dayton wouldn't find me. Kylian hadn't reached for me in anger. He couldn't make me tell the press. There would be no pictures, no alerts sent to Dayton's phone.

He won't find me. I'm safe. I silently repeated the mantra until I believed it, and the tension slowly drained out of me.

"How ya doing, sweetheart?"

I smiled at Val, the waitress who'd filled my coffee twice already. "I'm good, thanks."

"Want anything else? Or just more coffee?"

"One more."

"You stay here as long as you want, darling."

I smiled, grateful as she filled my cup to the brim. I added creamer and stirred until the coffee was a caramel color. *Calm down. He won't find me.*

CHAPTER SEVEN

KYLIAN

I turned down another street, looking for Gia after she stormed out of the condo. The droning sports station host I had on in the background cut out when my phone rang. I hit Accept before checking who it was, hoping it was her—worry eating at me because I'd caught her skittish reaction to the loud noise and it hadn't sat well with me. Something had happened to that girl, and she was clearly suffering ill effects.

"It's about time you answered me, Kylian."

Fuck. It was Dad. I slowed then pulled over to the curb. "I've been busy. Are you calling to find out how much Mom's treatment costs so you can help?"

Something rustled, then a door shut, and I knew he'd done that so his very young wife wouldn't hear him refuse to help. Jillian, Dad's wife, wasn't a bad person. She'd just hitched herself to a corrupt and much older one. And I already knew she didn't like the idea of Mom suffering if Dad could help in some way.

"I've gone above and beyond to help your mom," Dad growled. "I got her into that new treatment, which was no easy feat."

"Yeah, you did, and we're both grateful for that. The problem is she might not be able to stay in it if we can't pay the bills."

"Your mom is no longer my responsibility. That's what divorce is all about, but if you want me to help, you know what you can do for me."

"Are you kidding me?" I slammed my palm on the steering wheel. "You have more than enough money. Helping Mom wouldn't put a dent in Jillian's shopping allowance." A low blow against her, but it was true.

"You better watch your tone about your stepmother."

My stomach clenched in distaste. "She's five years older than me. And I already have a mother. One who's dying—and you could do something about it." My gut cramped. I felt sick. *Why can't I make him see the big picture?* "I'm running out of money. I can't pay for more treatments. We need your help." It killed me to ask him for anything.

"As I've said before, you know how to get it."

"Fuck you, Dad. I'm not dating some contributor's daughter to keep the funds rolling in for your campaign." I didn't wait for his response, hitting the end call button on the dash with more force than necessary.

He wouldn't help without significant strings attached, and dating whoever that girl was would lead to marriage. It'd already been dropped casually in conversation with him, and the pressure was getting worse each time we spoke. I wouldn't put it past him to announce my engagement to the press before I'd even gone on a date with whatever wealthy, entitled girl had her sights set on me so he could get what he wanted.

Dad expected me to trade my freedom for money. And I gladly would if I had no other options to save Mom's life. But I did—I just needed an invite to the combine, and I would enter the draft early.

CHAPTER EIGHT

GIA

My spoon clinked against the saucer as the diner's bell chimed. The air felt electrically charged, as if a storm was rolling in. I didn't even have to look up. I knew it was him. Awareness tingled on the back of my neck. My senses heightened but not like they had with the panic attack. I didn't know why, but I felt him when he was near. Before Kylian, I'd never experienced anything like it. With him, it just was.

He folded his large body into the seat across from me. Val zeroed in on him, but he declined to order anything. Then she was gone, and it was just us. He was heated. His shoulders were tense, and the muscle along his jaw jumped. I set down the spoon and lifted my eyes to meet his. I wouldn't speak first. It didn't matter. I didn't have long to wait before he spoke.

"I've been looking for you for hours." He waited for a beat.

I didn't respond.

"Come back with me. I want to talk about everything. Explain."

I shook my head no.

"We have a contract," he growled in a low voice, so only I could hear him. "You signed it. Are you backing out?"

I sighed, not wanting to play games. "Please. I would have to be a fool to give up on free rent. And I don't want to play a part in messing with your mom's hope and well-being. I know how much you love her, especially if you're willing to come to a crazy agreement with a virtual stranger." He wouldn't hurt his mom, and if I backed out, I would be a part in doing just that. "I'm fine with your parents knowing, but we didn't agree to anything public. I don't owe you anything." I whispered it, but the impact could have been a bomb going off with how his expression changed from open to shuttered.

"I disagree. That should stay on the table as an option."

Fuck that. I slammed my hand down flat against the table, making the silverware jump and rattle. "Too bad. No public announcement about our engagement." I worried that he might go ahead and let reporters know to further his endgame, and it was a reminder that another man was trying to run my life.

The only reason I hadn't told him to go straight to hell and caught the next bus out of Chicago was because I'd met his mom. She was so welcoming and kind, and on top of that, the way he acted toward her had gotten to me. One of the carefully erected walls I kept around my heart for survival had a hairline fracture in it because of that.

His situation tugged at my heart, making him more human than Dayton had ever pretended to be. But I was no fool. Publicly announcing our engagement would risk bringing my worst mistake to my doorstep. I needed something more if I was going to stay with Kylian and aid the jock-ass in his scheme.

I slid out of the booth. "Fine. Let's go talk."

CHAPTER NINE

KYLIAN

We entered my condo quietly, since it was the middle of the night. Back in my room, I paced the length of it. I had school, practice, and several other obligations the next day, and I'd spent hours I didn't have to spare looking for Gia. She was driving me crazy. "We need a rule that neither of us walks until the contract comes to its natural conclusion."

"Then don't push me on a public announcement."

"Look, I don't like our arrangement any more than you do, but we're both getting something out of it, so deal with it." I paused and, with great effort, shoved aside my animosity toward her, instead scrutinizing everything she wasn't saying.

She'd moved across the room and lain in the middle of my bed. *Is she finally getting comfortable with me?* She appeared relaxed, with her long, toned legs stretched out and crossed at the ankles. But her full lips pressed tightly together and the tense set of her shoulders as she leaned against my headboard told me more than her words.

"What are you hiding? Because trust me, the press will get a picture of us together, if they haven't already." They would dig into her life too.

I'd seen a reporter hanging around when we'd first arrived. I thought she'd noticed because her hand had gone up, but maybe it had just been in reaction to the flash of light.

"Why would you think I'm hiding something? I went to your mom's, didn't I?"

"Look, Gia." Frustration itched along my skin. She wasn't the only one with secrets. I hadn't told her about the pressure from my dad. "I've got a long day tomorrow and need to sleep. Can we agree that neither of us is going to walk early? That you won't take off on me and get caught looking upset by an eager reporter with a camera? Because it'll happen, then my mom, who doesn't believe us yet, will have even more unnecessary stress."

"Okay." A puff of air left her mouth. "I'll agree to honor the contract and not take off on you. I'm doing this for your mom because she doesn't need more bullshit. But I won't opt into a photoshoot."

"Whatever. We can talk about it more tomorrow. I need to sleep, and it would be much easier if you crashed here tonight."

"I don't—" The color drained from her face.

"Nothing will happen." *What is her problem?* "It's a king-sized bed. If you want to, you can put a wall of pillows between us." *I could take the couch, but why?* As soon as my head hit the pillow, I would pass out.

"Fine."

After her reluctant agreement, we took turns getting ready for bed. I loaned her a T-shirt to sleep in, hit the lights, and passed the fuck out.

The shrill beep of my phone's alarm woke me all too soon. Blindly, I slapped the phone until it stopped. It was too early. For another few minutes, I lay there, orienting myself. Neither of us had breached the wall of pillows Gia had built, but I was all too aware of her body on the other side. That girl was a puzzle I needed to figure out, but it would be better if I didn't.

So much tension and distrust stood between us. And I hated the fact that I wanted her.

"You awake?" I whispered in the dark room.

"Yeah, kind of hard not to be after your loud-ass alarm went off."

I grunted in agreement—I wasn't sorry it had woken her. "Get up if you want a ride back to the harbor. I've got a run this morning and class."

"This is inhumane."

"Nespresso and coffee pods are in the kitchen."

She grumbled then threw the covers off, somehow flinging them onto me. I tracked her slender form as she went toward the kitchen. I needed to get her—and how we hadn't agreed on anything other than that we would both stick with the deal until the tragic end—out of my mind.

I showered and got dressed before joining her in the kitchen. She had on one of my practice shirts, which fell to midthigh. Her long, dark hair had that just-fucked look, and it took everything in me not to drag her back to bed. I regretted not negotiating more into our contract.

She lifted a mug to her lips, eyes at half-mast and sexy as hell. "Coffee?"

Fuck my life. "No time." I needed to keep my head on straight. I had class then practice. Nothing else in the world mattered more than football and my mom's health. I couldn't let this girl, or how I wanted to do so many things to her, get in the way of my goals. But we did need to practice touching, since Mom was already suspicious and the whole act was about her happiness. Same with going pro early.

After that last round of bills from her treatment and my dad's refusal to chip in any more unless I agreed to his demands, I'd finally decided to put off graduating. Once I went pro, we would be free from relying on Dad's blackmail to pay for her treatments. "Need a ride?"

"No. I'll take the bus or, um, maybe call an Uber."

I kissed the top of her head on the way to the door, inhaling her vanilla and honey scent, then hightailed it out of there, an unsettling feeling chasing me the entire way. How natural kissing her felt was weird as fuck.

School and football were what I needed. Better than thinking about the ridiculousness of my life. I had three classes, and I plowed through them after grabbing a to-go coffee. Practice was next. I entered the spacious locker room to the familiar sounds of guys talking and laughing. I nodded to a few teammates then took my place next to Ares and Liam, who were already inside. I sat on the bench and tied my cleats as Ares tugged his practice jersey over his pads.

Liam took a seat next to me, already dressed. "What's up with the girl? I saw her early this morning. Is she gonna be a regular thing?"

I glared, irrationally angry that he might have seen her barely dressed. I should have thought about that before I left. His morning class started later than mine. "Yeah, she is."

"What's up with that, man? You don't usually hit a jersey chaser twice."

"Shut up about her. Not a jersey chaser." I scrubbed my hands over my face, not liking the complication, but I needed to let them in on the agreement between Gia and me. "I'll explain later."

"She took off before we left for class." Ares leaned against the lockers, his gaze boring into mine.

"Get on the field now!" Coach crossed the locker room on the way to the field, clipboard in hand.

"Thanks, Ares." I pushed off the bench to my feet and headed out with Ares and Liam.

As soon as we hit the field, my problems faded. It was always like that with football. I warmed up with Liam and Ares. Liam, my go-to wide receiver, ran the new routes, while Ares worked the kinks out of a few trick plays.

I'd met with Coach last week to develop three new plays for our arsenal. Our plays had crazy, varied names that required a lot of memorizing for all of us. On top of homework and watching film to prepare for upcoming games, it took a massive amount of time. I gladly invested everything I had into it, except what I reserved for Mom. Dinners and occasions when she needed help with doctor visits or care after treatments were nonnegotiable and something I'd worked out with Coach—to a degree. He would pull me if I started throwing interceptions or missed connections on the field.

Calvin, the second-string quarterback, fell into step with me. "Don't listen to what the fans are saying about the Michigan game. You're a good quarterback."

Fuck off. I wanted to say it, but that wasn't how I should lead my team. "I don't let random comments get to me."

"That's good. Especially the ones about your mom. That would get to anyone, but you're a rock. And that sweet piece the blog sites have a picture of, bet that helps take your mind off everything that's so far out of your control."

"Get on the fucking field, Calvin."

He laughed and jogged to the backup wide receivers to throw the football lobbed to him for a screen play.

Short of punching him, I couldn't go there with what Calvin had said about Mom, and that wouldn't help the team or me. It certainly wouldn't help Mom.

Would a picture of Gia and me out there be so bad? It might get my dad off my back. I threw a few passes, but thoughts of Gia were lodged in my head, which rarely happened on the field. I ground my teeth then overthrew a pass.

"Head in the game," Liam said under his breath before he took off running a route.

My head was so far from the game. It was stuck on Gia. She

was an anomaly, a fucking problem, really. I needed her to be a solution.

When we lined up and scrimmaged, my mind continued to wander—to Gia, my dad's demands for publicity to help him, and Mom's health. What I was usually able to block out broke through and screwed with my head. I threw passes short or too long. I mixed up the direction of a new play.

"Wilder!" Coach bellowed from the sideline.

I ground my teeth, yanked off my helmet, and jogged to him.

"What's going on?" Coach Becket's mustache worked overtime with the aggressive way he chewed his nicotine gum.

"Nothing, Coach." Frustration buzzed through my veins. No way would I unload everything to him. "Nothing I can't handle."

"I know you've got a lot on your plate with your mom's illness, Wilder, but if you can't get your head on straight for Bama's game, I'll have to bench you."

"Understood." I dragged my arm across my forehead, swiping some sweat away. "I'll get control of it."

"See that you do."

I cringed at the shrill sound of Coach's whistle as he signaled the end of practice. Several teammates clapped me on the shoulder or back as they passed by for the locker room.

"You've got this, Wilder," Marc, the other tight end, said.

"Get whatever girl is messing with the game under you and out of your mind," Steve, our center, growled as he slapped me on the back.

If only it were that simple. I uncurled my fists, wishing it weren't the end of my time on the field. I needed to get back in the zone. Gia breaking through was unacceptable. Luckily, we had a line of demarcation that would not be crossed, symbolized by her pillow barricade. It was a damn good thing she lived on the boat.

Ares fell into step at my side, Liam just ahead of us as we entered the building.

"You were off your game, and the only difference I could see was that chick," Liam said over his shoulder. "You need to do something to get her out of your head. Tap that, quit it, and kick her to the curb for good. You have too much riding on the next few games."

"You have no idea what you're talking about." I got where Liam was coming from, though. During my first two years in college, I had been a player too. But never at his level. I cared about football and training more than partying or hooking up. Liam never slept with the same girl twice.

"A decisive win against Alabama could put you in a position to go pro without waiting for the draft," Ares reminded me. "Florida and Philadelphia need a new quarterback, and I've heard they're looking at you hard."

"I'm not going to fuck up that game."

"Then what's going on?" Ares yanked off his jersey and tossed it into his bag. "It's not like you to let anything throw off your game. But, man"—Ares glanced a few lockers over, dropping his voice so no one else could hear—"if Calvin leaks anything to the press about your performance today, he'll spin it that you're not stable or mature enough for an NFL contract."

I threw my cleat harder than necessary. It thudded against the back of my locker. Calvin Fucking Matthews had been gunning for QB1 ever since I took over the spot my first year, when the former quarterback went on IR with a ruptured Achilles tendon.

It wasn't going to happen. Calvin didn't have the talent I did, or the ability to lead.

Still, I needed to do something to circumvent any more problems, and more would come. Because I knew how Calvin operated, and it wasn't an if—it was a when. His social media presence was an issue. I glared in his direction, noting how he was already flapping his gums, live streaming some bullshit he shouldn't. I knew what I had to do—eliminate any damage

Calvin inflicted because of my "marriage" to Gia. Steady and mature wouldn't be an issue.

Many coaches preferred their players to have stable home lives. Not that it was a deciding factor for recruits, but it wouldn't hurt. It was why I needed to announce our engagement publicly. Decision made, I finished dressing in gym clothes to hit the weights. On the way out, I ran into Siobhan, a reporter for Baller News Blog, and gave her the tip that should help buffer me from multiple problems, just as my phone rang.

Dad. His timing just fucking figured.

CHAPTER TEN

GIA

I took the bus to Kylian's mom's apartment and, after climbing the stairs, stood in front of her door, laden with groceries. On the run for so many months, I'd gotten good at finding bargains. And while I hated spending even a dime of the money Kylian gave me for living expenses, I didn't mind sharing some with his mom. No matter how much I didn't want to ask him for more, I would eventually have to because I had to squirrel away every little bit I could in case I needed to go on the run again—which was why I took the bus there and would walk home. Ubers were expensive.

Before I knocked, I slipped the engagement ring into my pocket. She didn't know about it yet, and I didn't want to be the one to tell her. It took a few minutes before the door opened and Evalyn stood in front of me. Deep circles etched the skin under her eyes, and her shoulders curled in.

I pasted a bright smile on my face. "Hi, Evalyn. I hope you don't mind me stopping by unexpectedly." I lifted the groceries a little to draw her eye to them. "I thought I could do some meal prep for you."

"Oh, Gia. Of course. It's so nice to see you." She opened the door wide and stepped to the side to make room. "Come on in."

"Thanks." I lifted the bags slightly. "Mind if I go straight to the kitchen?"

"Go right ahead." She reached for one of the bags. "Here, let me help."

"It's fine. I've got it." The last thing I wanted was to use any of her energy.

I came to make things easier for her. Kylian had shared his schedule with me. It was insane. Most mornings, he ran with his teammates at the crack of dawn, followed by team meetings or strength and conditioning, classes, football practice, and dinner somewhere in there. Then, he used whatever time was left for homework or his mom. And I got the feeling he did his best to spend the most time with her. With everything on his shoulders, I suspected she wasn't getting as much help as she needed.

I set the groceries on the counter by the sink and started unloading. "Did you have lunch?" It was close to that time, and I hoped I'd caught her before she'd made anything.

"No. I didn't have a taste for anything."

"What about a smoothy?" I'd done some research before walking to the grocery store about what cancer patients should eat to help their immune systems and strength. It was basically a whole lot of vegetables and fruit. There were other things, too, and I would prep some plant-based meals as well as some chicken and fish.

"That sounds good. What can I do to help?"

I grinned over my shoulder as I filled the sink with cold water to wash the fruit and veggies. "Keep me company?" I had a plan. "Kylian's so busy, and I figured you might have more free time, like I do."

She showed me where the cutting board and blender were, and I got to work as she pulled out one of the kitchen chairs and sat. "You'll have to tell me how much all that cost so I can reimburse you."

"No need. Kylian paid for it."

"Oh, that was nice. And I'm glad you're here too. Watching TV can get old."

"I agree." I wouldn't confess that I wasn't working, and so far, she hadn't asked. I hoped to avoid anything too personal—other than stuff about my uncle. I liked to talk about him. It made me feel like he was close. I launched into a few stories about how he'd drawn me out of my angry shell after Mom had died and gotten me into the kitchen. In turn, she told me some hilarious ones about Kylian when he was young.

The repetitive motions of cutting the vegetables and putting them into containers soothed me, and I relaxed into the easy conversation. "Football was king on Sundays at our house. We used to prepare the menu during the week and make a feast. It was the only day Uncle Jimmy was a 49ers fan, and I volley between whatever team has the best offensive line, especially quarterbacks. So when Kansas City played the 49ers, we upped the competition in the house through food—his menu against mine."

"He sounds amazing. Was it just the two of you?"

I placed a green smoothy in front of her and returned to meal prepping. "Yeah. My grandparents had passed, and Uncle Jimmy was Mom's only brother. I'm lucky I got to have the time with him that I did."

"Gia."

I turned at the surprise in her voice, and a knowing smile curved my lips. "It's good, isn't it?" Very few people thought a smoothy consisting mostly of vegetables would taste delicious.

"It's amazing." She took another sip. "And now you're in trouble because I'll want one of these every day."

"I love them too." I separated a few containers. "Do you have any Post-it notes?"

"In the drawer to the left of the fridge."

I got them then wrote directions on each container. "These are easy to prepare, but I'm putting notes on everything so you can make whatever sounds good."

"You're an angel, Gia."

I jerked as my nerves took a hit from the term of endearment. Tingles traveled from my arms down to my hands, and the pen fell from my numb fingers.

"Are you okay?"

"Yeah, sorry." I bent to pick up the pen, grateful for the moment to get control of my reaction. "I think I'll make myself one of those too." I flipped the switch on the blender, filling the room with the whirling motor's noise. By the time it was done and I poured it into a glass, I was back to myself. I sat at the table with her, jumping into questions about what Kylian was like as a kid to distract her further.

It worked. She launched into one story after another. The more she talked, the better I felt. Spending time with Evalyn was just as therapeutic to me as I hoped it would be for her. When we finished our smoothies, I washed the dishes and put everything away.

I didn't want to overstay my welcome and made plans to come back the next day to do some cleaning, despite her initial protest. It didn't take much convincing on my part, and by the time I made it back to the boat, I had a solid plan to help and spend time with Kylian's mom.

CHAPTER ELEVEN

KYLIAN

I jogged up the four flights of stairs to Mom's apartment then let myself in with my key. With the door open, I stopped short at the sight of Mom and Gia sitting together on the couch, drinking tea.

"Ah, hey." I rubbed the back of my neck. "I didn't know you were coming by today, Gia." *What the heck is she doing here?*

"Hi." She smiled, if a little shyly. "I wasn't doing anything, so I figured I could stop by. I know we're coming for dinner tomorrow night, but I was free now, so… What are you doing here? I thought you had class today."

"The professor had an emergency, and it was cancelled. Skipping lunch gave me more time."

"Good." Mom grinned, looking refreshed and happy, which set me at ease over Gia being there. "Wait till you taste what Gia made us for lunch. It's in the kitchen. Get some, and bring it in here to eat with us."

"Okay." I was more confused than ever.

Gia excused herself to help me, and I followed.

In the kitchen, she dropped her voice to a whisper while she plated a chicken and vegetable dish. "Hey, I'm sorry I didn't tell you I was here." She shrugged then sank her teeth into her bottom lip before releasing it. "I just thought that since you're so busy, I could stop by and help your mom sometimes."

"Thank you." I touched her shoulder then let my hand drop to my side. "It means a lot to me."

"It's not a problem. I like your mom, and I miss my uncle. It's good for me too."

She was turning out to be so much more than I'd expected. To distract myself from how much I was softening toward her, I opened the fridge to grab a bottle of water and was greeted by rows of containers with Post-it notes. "Did Mom order a food service?"

"Ah, no. That was me."

"Really?" I pulled one out, impressed by what she'd done in such a short time. And Mom—she looked so happy. I rubbed my chest, trying to soothe the ache over how touched I was by Gia's actions. I put the food back, grabbed some water, then accepted the plate of food she held out with a hand devoid of jewelry.

"Wait, where's your ring?" A slight jolt of panic shot through me. *Had she lost it?* I hadn't told her, but the diamond ring had been my grandmother's. I took the plate from her and set it down on the counter.

"It's in my pocket. I assumed you would want us to tell her together."

I grinned. "I do, and thanks for thinking about what would mean the most to her."

She nodded, and an unexpected wave of longing filled me on the heels of my gratitude. It made me want to reach out and give her something too. "Hey, you know you can trust me." I got the feeling she didn't do that often—let people in, well, aside from my mom. "I would like to be your friend."

Her shoulders dropped about an inch, and she tilted her head back to look at me. "Thanks, I'd like that."

She was so damn pretty that I acted on instinct. My hand

cupped her cheek, and I leaned in to brush my lips over hers. But when Mom walked in, we both jerked apart.

Gia rushed over to take the teacup and saucer rattling in Mom's hand. "Did you need a refill?"

"That would be lovely." Mom squeezed her shoulder, then Gia became a flurry of motion, getting hot water from the kettle on the stove and steeping a new tea bag in the cup. She carried it into the other room for her, leaving Mom and me alone for a minute. I picked up my plate to follow Gia when Mom's hand on my arm stopped me.

"I really like her, Kylian. I mean, look at everything she's done for me."

"The meals?" I tipped my head toward the fridge, making a mental note to give Gia a credit card for groceries.

"She didn't want me to tell you, but yes. That and she's come over the past few days to clean and stay to chat. We'd planned to go for a walk to get some exercise later today." Tears misted Mom's eyes. "It's just so nice having her here."

I pulled her into my side, shocked and a little in awe of the person with whom I'd embarked on a fake relationship that felt more real by the second.

CHAPTER TWELVE

GIA

Two weeks had passed since the tense sleepover at Kylian's and him finding out that I'd been going to his mom's to help out. A shiver raced over me, and my fingers tightened on his steering wheel.

I hated how he affected me—I ached when he was near. All that delicious, tempting, sculpted muscle and my body turned into a wanton puddle of need. *And sleeping in the same bed?* It had taken me hours to drift off because I was so aware of him.

Good thing I'd quit men, or I would have scaled the ridiculous pillow wall and licked him from his washboard abs to his sinful lips, which I bet could do some pretty amazing things. But I wouldn't be seduced by his deep voice or how the brush of his hand along my back sent little jolts of electricity to my core.

Mentally, I wasn't ready to be with anyone, though he had some inexplicable hold on me. I had to keep that front and center in my mind, not how much I wanted to use him as a stress reliever. The only thing I liked about him so far was that he'd been a man of his word. I had to give it to him. The more time I spent with him, the more fissures invaded my walled-off heart, and a slow start to trust took root.

It was pretty sweet that he'd loaned me his vehicle, though I had to adjust the mirrors and move the seat forward, since it was set for a giant. Of course, a sports station droned through the speakers. I would have taken the bus, but Kylian had insisted I use his SUV to get groceries for the boat. As a bonus, I had his credit card, something I wasn't about to say no to.

I scanned the complicated dash at a light, wanting to change the radio to something with upbeat music. The light changed, and I returned my hand to the steering wheel, not comfortable with the controls yet.

The radio hosts murmured in the background as I kept pace with traffic, singing a song about controlling, vampiric men under my breath—the perfect description for Dayton, the life sucker. The asshole was never far from my thoughts. With each bar of the song, a sense of freedom wove around me until I was belting lyrics only I could hear.

I almost slammed on the brakes when I heard the sports guys mention Kylian's girlfriend. With my finger, I punched up the volume on the steering wheel to better hear the hosts, Joe and Brad.

"A few pictures show the new couple have been spotted around town," Joe said.

"How do we know that means anything, Joe? Kylian Wilder was also photographed with a Chicago Bulls cheerleader on Michigan Ave throughout a weekend."

"Sure, but that was almost two months ago."

"Both were posted on a fan blog, which isn't the most reliable," Brad said. "I don't think it's anything noteworthy. The latest headline was 'Kylian Wilder's New Girlfriend—Fraud or Fiancée?' It's all sensationalized. What matters is how he'll do in the game against Alabama. And if you check the backup quarterback's live streams, it does not sound good."

"Sure. Sure," Joe said. "I hear you on both counts. But I think the new girlfriend is noteworthy, especially with Wilder's comment about things being serious, along with a picture of them holding hands while she tried to shield her face from the camera."

"Whoa. Kylian Wilder made a statement? Oh, I see it now. Interesting."

"Yeah," Jo said. "Kylian Wilder declared things were getting serious with his girlfriend, Gia Mason, to a university reporter. I saw the write-up on Fall Lake University's Baller News Blog."

I'm going to kill him. I couldn't believe it. What a shit show. Changing lanes, I listened intently as I noticed a car riding my bumper, mimicking everything I did. A trickle of unease skated over me. Too many things were happening at once.

Brad's voice cut through my thoughts once more. "I'm not saying this is a hoax, but the timing is suspect with Danbury Wilder's senatorial campaign."

"Come on, Brad," Joe said. "That's a little far-fetched. If he is serious about this girl, that'll only help him in the long run, especially with the upcoming draft."

"I know some coaches prefer their players to be in a serious relationship, since there's less drama, but is it really a factor? I don't think so. This guy's stats speak for themselves."

I was so mad, I hit the dash a few times until the sound stopped. He may not have announced our fake engagement, but he'd put a spotlight on me regardless, even after I'd said no.

He was a dead man. I would tear him a new one when I dropped off his stupidly expensive SUV. My hands shook, and I gripped the wheel tight before turning onto a side street—the parking lot for the grocery store in sight. Only a block ahead, I put the turn signal on as a black sedan pulled alongside me. A phone rose, snapping a picture.

Goddammit!

Palms sweating, I yanked the wheel, bypassed the grocery store, and sped down another street. The sedan made a U-turn, cutting off another car in the process. Horns blared from pissed-off drivers. Fear sank its talons into my racing heart. *Who's following me? A reporter? Kylian's rabid fans? Or worse— someone working for Dayton?*

With the steady increase in rush hour traffic, I estimated the boat to be approximately half an hour away. That wouldn't work. I would be a fool to lead them there. Instead, I merged onto the highway, weaving through traffic as space opened. I glanced in the mirror, hoping I'd lost them. I hadn't. The sedan mimicked my moves. Sweat coated my palms, and tears pricked the corners of my eyes. *Where could I go?* I needed to be and feel safe. Invisible. Fucking Kylian.

My teeth gnawed on my lower lip as ideas came and went. A police station would be the smartest. Whoever was following me would be stupid to follow me into a cop shop. But for real, I couldn't go there—it was too risky.

At the last minute, I swerved across two lanes and took the next exit, barely making it. The cacophony of horns and screeching tires told me everything I needed to know. The car was still on my tail.

My gaze ping-ponged from street names to stores and parking garages and finally landed on Kylian's athletic pass in the cupholder. A partially hysterical laugh burst from me. I bet they couldn't follow me into the athletic parking lot on campus.

It wasn't far. I floored it, my foot slamming down on the pedal when I could. The tires squealed as I took a turn too fast and tight. *Come on. Come on.* Sweat beaded along my hairline. Ten feet, and I would be there. Students walked to and from classes, and some neared the upcoming crosswalk. I had to slow down. The sensation of hundreds of red ants crawling over my skin accompanied each wasted second.

My mind raced with all that could go wrong. I yanked the wheel and jerked to a stop at the athletic lot's entrance. With my finger, I hit the button to lower the window automatically, scooped up Kylian's card, and waved it at the scanner. The gate swung up, and I crawled forward. I didn't move more than a few inches past until the gate went back down. I wouldn't chance them trying to shoot through the security after I'd gotten in and the gate was still up.

With a shaky exhalation, I eased the SUV forward and headed down one aisle, glancing at my mirrors to keep track of the sedan. They slowed then parked along the curb near the entrance to the gated lot. I was truly screwed.

On top of all that, I didn't have my phone. I'd left it some-where—probably the boat, maybe at Kylian's place. I hadn't gotten my groceries, which was the least of my worries. And I was trapped. If I tried to leave, whoever waited in that car would resume following me. I needed to park somewhere they couldn't get clear pictures and maybe where I could see Kylian leave the building after practice. I racked my brain to remember when he said he would be done for the day.

I slowed to a stop and thumped my forehead on the steering wheel. He'd gotten a ride from his roommates so I could use his car. I hadn't paid attention to what he'd said. *Did he even tell me when he'd be back?* I didn't think so. We could barely get through a single day together without arguing, despite the attraction. The only time we had to fake that we were in a relationship was around his mom.

I couldn't do anything but sit and hope Kylian came out and saw me. Inhaling a deep breath, I pulled up along the curb to the athletic building's entrance, shut off the motor, and slumped in my seat to wait.

The reality of my situation weighed a ton. I was cornered, despite the fifty-thousand-dollar contract I'd signed with Kylian. And I had no way to call him for help.

CHAPTER THIRTEEN

KYLIAN

I met the car Dad had sent at a side door of the stadium, an unfortunate result of answering the call from him a few days ago. The driver made a quick stop at the condo, where I changed into a suit and tie, then got back in the vehicle and was driven to the off-camera fundraiser for Dad's political campaign.

That was how Dad billed it, but I didn't believe him for one second. He pressured me until we'd struck a deal on the phone that he would pay for Mom's following two treatments so long as I showed up at his fundraiser event. I was his show pony so the world could see Danbury Wilder as a family man who'd raised a talented son with NFL potential. It was a way to get his name circulating in the media more and remind people of his relevance in the upcoming elections.

When I exited the car in front of the venue, several reporters converged as far as the red velvet ropes allowed, shouting questions.

"Kylian, do you support your father in the upcoming election?"

"What do you think your chances are with the draft? Do you hope to stay local?"

"Who was the girl you were photographed with over the weekend?"

I smiled, my teeth clenched so hard I worried they would crack, and I didn't answer a single question shouted my way, no matter how much I wanted to reply to that last one. A few people ahead of me slowed my path to the door and my escape from the vultures.

That was when I saw him—my father—at the entrance with several other older men accompanied by a few ladies dripping with diamonds. It was his chance to show me off and impress his cronies, particularly Harland Maxwell Honeycutt, the older, portly man puffing on a cigar and standing to Dad's right.

A younger woman broke free from their group and hurried toward me. I'd never met her, but she seemed to know me. The reporters zeroed in on her, tracking her every move.

Her bright-red lips curved into a wide, somewhat strained smile, and she wore black-framed trendy glasses that made her look like a sexy librarian. Her golden-blond hair had been twisted into some fancy updo, and her gold dress molded to her as she wove through the guests before stopping at my side. "Kylian, I've been waiting for you."

She grabbed my tie and pulled with shocking strength, getting me to bend more out of surprise than anything. Soft red lips planted themselves on mine, and her hand gripped the back of my neck as she pressed her body against me. *Goddammit.* My hands automatically went to her hips, and as my senses returned, I broke the kiss, moving her back to put some space between us. I fought the need to shove her away while the reporters' energy went up a notch.

Forced laughter spilled from her as she slipped her arm in mine and tugged. "Come on. Daddy has been waiting to talk to you." She flattened a hand on my chest. "But I wanted a moment alone with you first."

Cameras flashed around us, capturing the setup I knew the situation to be. Her daddy had to be none other than the deep-pocketed Honeycutt, which made her his daughter and the one my father wanted me to date and then marry—Melanie Honeycutt.

I bent near her ear so only she could hear. "I know what game you're playing, and trust me, nothing will come of it."

"We'll see about that." She matched my tone, determination bright in her deep-brown eyes heavily framed by fake eyelashes. She slipped her arm possessively around mine and clung like the vulture I guessed her to be.

"I don't have anything to offer you," I said. "I don't know what our fathers have promised, but you're better off with an up-and-coming hedge-fund millionaire."

"Oh, darling." She leaned against my arm, more laughter tinkling into the night and drawing notice from the press. "I've dated them and have no interest. But the wife of an NFL quarterback who has a bright future like you do? Sign me up."

"Nothing is guaranteed in life." We were on the stairs, farther from the press but closing in on my snake of a father and hers.

"I'm a woman who knows what she wants. And athletes like you have stamina and staying power. You'll make history, and I'll be right beside you."

Ambitious. I knew her type. Jersey chasers were a dime a dozen, but wealthy ones were dangerous. Melanie Honeycutt was a woman with the right name who would agree to the perfect number of children and the house on the correct street and would soccer-mom her way into the PTA Hall of Fame. She was ideal for the right guy or athlete, but that wasn't me. I'd grown up with my dad using us. I didn't want that in my wife.

I got the irony in that statement. It didn't matter. Deep down, I sensed Gia wasn't a snake.

"There's my superstar." Dad's smile stretched his face as he clapped me on the back.

"Kylian, so glad you could make it." Cigar smoke leaked behind Harland's slightly yellowed teeth, curling past his white mustache.

I shook his extended hand. "Mr. Honeycutt."

The rest of the men introduced themselves and their wives as we headed inside and toward the area where tables were set up. I knew the drill, since I'd been forced to attend a few of these events in the past while Dad was making his debut in politics.

Soft music played in the background from the string quartet behind a podium where speeches would be made. Waiters and waitresses dressed in black-and-white formal wear wove through the guests, carrying trays of champagne. Melanie helped herself to one, her talons still firmly on my bicep.

I escorted her to the table our group circled and held out a chair for her. With a bright smile that assumed victory, she sat. After I scooted her chair in, I escaped, making my way through the crowd and mingling. How that would help my father become the next Illinois senator was beyond me, but I had no choice.

After an hour and before dinner, I found Dad and indicated for him to follow me to a quiet corner of the room. I tapped my phone's ride-share app then shoved the device in my pocket and studied him as he approached. We shared the same athletic build and jawline, but I had two inches on him. Gray peppered his dark-brown hair, giving him a distinguished air.

"Melanie is wonderful, isn't she? The perfect match and the right bloodline."

I snorted at his audacity to think such bullshit. "As opposed to ours? Mom's family had more money than yours. What's the point here, Dad?"

"The point, son"—Dad's eyes hardened, and the muscle on

his jaw ticked like mine did when I was frustrated—"is that she would make an advantageous wife."

"Melanie isn't the kind of woman who needs to be set up. She's not unfortunate looking and can hold a conversation. But she's not for me." I was done with the charade. "I did what you demanded. Showed up, mingled, and talked to as many people as possible. I trust you'll hold up your end of the bargain and pay for Mom's next two treatments."

"I told you I needed you to schmooze Honeycutt. I'm sure you don't want your poor, sick mother living on the street."

"That would make a fantastic headline, Dad. 'Senatorial candidate Danbury Wilder threatens his son to cooperate or he'll toss his sick ex-wife out of her apartment.' Bet that would win you tons of points in the polls."

"Don't you threaten me, son."

"That was your game plan tonight, not mine. I did what you said. Don't mess with Mom. Make those payments, and I'll keep my mouth shut." My phone buzzed, indicating my ride had arrived. "Good night."

I turned and left, ignoring the camera flash as I hurried down the stairs to the waiting car.

Inside the vehicle, I sat back, relaxed, and closed my eyes. Melanie Honeycutt had been all over me, and the reporters had witnessed the scene she'd orchestrated. Clearly, the information I'd slipped to the college's blogger hadn't circulated enough, and it wasn't the time for me to make a public announcement. If I'd done that at the fundraiser, Dad would've made Mom suffer.

What a train wreck. And Gia… I could imagine what the morning's headline would be. I needed to get to her before she read it online.

Now that the Honeycutts were sinking their claws into me in exchange for backing my father's campaign, it'd become more apparent that I had to keep Mom from getting hurt. I just needed a bit of leverage.

CHAPTER FOURTEEN

GIA

Stationed front and center at the stadium entrance wasn't an option for long, especially after the pressure in my bladder became unbearable. I'd parked, grabbed my purse, and hurried inside to hide from the reporter as a group of athletes exited—none of them Kylian or his roommates. A sinking feeling settled in my stomach that I might have missed him.

I aimlessly wandered the halls until I found a restroom and a room with a couch, a small table and chairs, vending machines, and a TV. I hadn't memorized his number, and I had no way to call him without my phone. I'd been in worse positions, both before and after I'd left Dayton. At least I had a few dollars in my purse and could get snacks, but what I wouldn't give for a caramel latte. Water and a granola bar would have to do.

I stretched out on the blue couch, worked the kinks from my neck, then grabbed the remote. After channel surfing and not finding anything I wanted to watch, curiosity got the best of me, and I toggled over to the TV's internet app then used the remote to type in the Baller News Blog. It wasn't my best moment, and I shouldn't have given in to reading the gossip site, but I had time to kill.

I downed half my water and the entire granola bar before I looked at the screen to see a video of my fake boyfriend walking into some fancy-schmancy venue. The blond bimbo next to him looked more like Science-Nerd Barbie than the Malibu version her platinum hair said she was trying for. *What the actual fuck?* My bottle of water tumbled to the floor as I jerked forward to get a closer look from my spot on the couch.

The bimbo's bright-red lips planted on Kylian's—*lucky bitch.* My eyes were glued to the screen, and I held my breath, which I released in a huff when he didn't push her away. A growl rumbled from my throat as a rush of possessiveness swept over me in a jealous haze.

Vision tunneled on the TV, I jerked to my feet and moved closer. I shouldn't care. We were business partners. But dammit, I did. He was sort of a jerk but so freaking kind too. And. He. Was. Mine. *Sort of.* By contract, he was.

I twisted the engagement ring around my finger. We weren't even to the part of his plan where we were married. But it was his endgame, his gift to his mom. *And yet he's letting Science-Nerd Barbie rub all over him?* He was breaking paragraph three— cheating. And paragraph three had been his fucking idea.

I clicked off the TV, having seen enough. I was fired up and not going to wait inside hiding any longer. I'd managed to get that far on my own. I refused to let some idiot reporter camped outside stop me from confronting the cheating bastard.

Yanking the door hard, I stormed into the hallway and toward the exit. A group of girls towered over me. Judging by their clothes, probably basketball players. Perfect. I knew how to merge with and get lost in a crowd. We passed through the heavy doors and left the building without incident. Once in the parking lot, I broke free, two rows over from where I'd parked Kylian's vehicle. After slipping past the few vehicles left in the lot, I quickly unlocked the SUV and climbed in.

Doors locked and my purse stowed in the console, I looked

across the lot to where the photographer had parked. He was still there, but his head rested against his window. He was probably asleep—one thing was finally going my way. Perfect.

I drove out of the lot with a swipe of Kylian's athletic card and past the sleeping reporter. I headed straight to his condo but changed directions when I realized I couldn't get into his place. That needed to change—if we continued the farce he had legally set in motion.

When I arrived at the marina, I parked, looked around to make sure no reporters had followed me, then got out. The dark water gently lapping at the boats was calm, unlike my volatile mood. I jogged through the harbor and along the pier where his boat was tethered. Once on board, I let myself into the cabin and flipped on the galley light, illuminating the smooth teak cabinets and floor. The door to the primary room was open, and I went in, expecting to launch myself on the bed. Only Kylian was sprawled across the mattress, still gorgeous in his formal wear, asleep.

I took a minute to study how peaceful he looked while taking up the majority of the space before I pulled the pillow out from beneath his head and smacked him across the face with it.

"What the fuck?" He yanked the pillow away.

I fell onto him from the force of his grab. Quickly scrambling off, I fought the unwanted snap of electricity from where our bodies touched. But what shocked me to my core was the lack of fear. Normally, a quick move like he'd made would've sent me spiraling into my personal hell—none of that had happened. I shoved the thoughts aside and stored them for later scrutiny. One thing was glaringly clear—I trusted him. At least, I did with my physical well-being. But he had something to answer for, and I refused to let him get away with it. "You violated the contract, cheater."

"I didn't cheat." He scowled fiercely as he sat up. "I came here looking for you. Where've you been all night?"

Arms crossed over my chest, I scowled. "You lost the right to ask me that when you got down with Bill Nye the Science Guy's daughter."

His lips briefly twitched at the corners, which only made me angrier. It wasn't a laughing matter. And why was I harping on that when what I should be arguing with him about was what he'd said to the college blogger?

"I wasn't getting down with anyone." His deep voice rumbled.

"There's evidence," I snapped, cursing my traitorous core's reaction to his voice.

He stayed quiet for a moment. His eyes closed briefly, and a puff of air left his firm lips. "It's bullshit. There's no evidence because I didn't do a damned thing. I had to go to the fundraiser—"

"I'm not a fool. I know what I saw." Through gritted teeth, I spelled it out for him. "She may have kissed you, but you didn't push her away. And she hung all over you. There are so many pictures." I clamped my lips shut, horrified at how my voice wavered toward the end. *What was that?*

Softer, he said, "You have no reason to be insecure or jealous."

I held up my hand against the absurdity of his assumption. "I'm not either of those things. I don't like being made a fool of." I shook my head, working hard to maintain composure. "You don't belong to me anyway, despite stupid paragraph three. We can dissolve the contract. Go get Science-Nerd Barbie. I'm sure she would happily be in a fake relationship with you. All you need to do is pay me the money you owe me, and I'm gone."

He moved fast. Steel arms wrapped around me. I gasped at the feel of his body flush against mine as he pulled me onto the bed with him.

I'd sworn off men for good. *Why does he have to affect me so much that I want to toss my prior vow to the curb?* The weight of the ring on my finger and the near kiss at his mom's taunted me. *Do I care about him more than I thought? How did that happen?*

"We're in this together. I'm sorry about what happened with Melanie. It was a tricky situation, one I'll avoid in the future by making sure you're by my side if I have to go to any more of those events."

"That's not the only thing. You told a blogger you were in a relationship with me. You gave her my name after I'd told you not to do that."

"Technically, I didn't go against what you said, which was to not announce our engagement."

"It still counts." I needed to check again to make sure Dayton was where he needed to stay—back in California. I would do a deep internet dive when I was alone.

He studied my face, his gaze bouncing between my eyes. "You're right. I'm sorry. I was trying to handle a few situations, and it was the wrong way to go about it."

I worried my lip for a few seconds before shrugging. "Fine. But know I'm not happy about it. Not at all."

His big hand smoothed down my back, and I slowly relaxed into his touch, the sucker that I was. His other hand tilted my chin so our eyes met. As his fingers traced the side of my cheek, those unwanted tingles erupted, and I couldn't suppress the shiver that time. Shoving aside what I'd witnessed on TV, I thought about how he showed he cared.

"I do belong to you, for now. I'm yours, and you're mine. Period."

Despite the noted time restraint, my traitorous mind and body melted. I was too tired to fight how he made me ache every time he touched me. My hungry gaze locked on his lips. Maybe it was time to find out what it would be like to kiss him.

CHAPTER FIFTEEN

KYLIAN

Gia's gaze found my lips, and I couldn't deny how much I wanted her. Each day with her, it was harder than the last to keep my hands to myself. She was still angry. I couldn't blame her. I was too. Part of me longed for jealousy to be what had prompted her strong reaction to Melanie. I didn't know what I would have done if the roles were reversed. Probably smashed the guy's face in.

I slid my hand along the slender curve of her neck to cup her nape, drawing her closer, testing for resistance. There was none. She came willingly, and I felt like I'd won.

A shiver of anticipation raced through me as I lifted my head toward hers. I wanted to taste her lips more than my next breath. Her eyelids fluttered closed as my lips grazed hers. She returned my kiss. Soft at first, tentative. When her arms wrapped around my neck, her fingers buried in my hair, I deepened the kiss, devouring her lips, reveling in her taste. Her response was instantaneous. The passion between us was electric, explosive. I angled her head, tasting her fully. *So fucking sweet.* When she shifted her hips, creating friction, I strained to push into her, hating the clothing barrier.

A moan slipped from her throat, reverberating through me and unleashing any restraint I thought I had. I needed her, and my control was threadbare. But it was our first kiss, and I fought my insatiable hunger and eased back. My breath crashed against hers.

I traced the curve of her soft cheek, a swell of possessiveness flaring in me at the sight of her kiss-swollen lips. Her lids rose, gifting me a view of her dazed bright-blue eyes.

"I've tried to deny how you make me feel. Gia, after that kiss, I can't. I want you, but I won't push you to do more than you're ready for."

Gia

I trembled at the way Kylian looked at me. Butterflies erupted in my stomach. I'd wanted to do this for myself, and the way he made me feel could keep me warm at night when I had to move on eventually. I trusted him. The decision was made, and I eased back on the mattress, creating much-needed distance between us. He reluctantly released me.

On shaky legs, I stood at the edge of the bed and whipped off my shirt then shimmied out of my leggings, needing the control. It was my decision, and making it sent a wave of power surging through me. "I want you too."

He practically levitated off the bed and was in front of me in a flash. I sucked in a breath and willed my body's fight-or-flight to cease and desist.

He noted my flinch and paused. "What is it?" His hands stilled from undoing his shirt's buttons.

I shook my head, hating how specific movements brought unbridled fear. It was a learned behavior bestowed on me from Dayton. But he wasn't there, and I wasn't afraid of Kylian—not like that. He wouldn't hurt me physically. The uncontrollable learned response just hit me at times. Intimacy didn't scare me, only certain fast movements that triggered me. I straightened my spine and shoved away the remnants of my urge to flee as I lost myself in the sight of the incredible man and athlete before me. Concern swam through his expressive eyes.

"You just startled me. I'm okay." I laid my hand on his chest, refusing to let Dayton come between us or my decision to be with Kylian. "Promise."

Kylian didn't move, his gaze dancing over my face. "Gia, we don't have to do anything. I don't want to pressure you."

His willingness to stop, no matter how hard he was—I'd noted the way he strained against his zipper—warmed me. How he'd felt moments ago, pressed against me, chased the last of my chill away. I shook my head and eased closer. My fingers deftly undid the first few buttons of his shirt before I let my gaze meet and hold his. I let him see my desire burning for him.

"Only if you're sure." He closed what remained of the distance between us and rested his hand over my fluttering pulse at the base of my neck.

My lips parted as I eased his shirt from his shoulders. The feel of his skin, all that corded muscle bunching and flexing beneath my touch, quickened my breath. All I could do was nod.

Another second passed before he gave in with a groan then bent and trailed kisses from my jawline down my neck while I explored the well-defined contours of his chest, the skin taut under my touch. He tore the rest of his clothes off then peeled my panties from my body.

He turned us, and the mattress pressed at the back of my thighs. As if I weighed nothing, he lifted me then laid me on the bed, his hungry gaze heating every inch of me.

"You're so beautiful."

He joined me, and with excruciating slowness, his hand moved up the outer side of my thigh. His lips captured mine, brushing back and forth until I moaned, and he deepened the kiss. I slid my hand around his back, urging him closer, the sensations addictive.

I explored his body in the silvery moonlight streaming through the porthole, desperate to experience all of him. I moaned, quivering with need as he broke our kiss only to press his lips to my thundering pulse. His teeth scraped the sensitive skin on my neck. I panted from his every caress. His large hands cupped my ass, and he ground his length against my core. I cried out from the delicious pressure, hooking a leg over his hip. He was close to my entrance but didn't give in, no matter how much I squirmed.

He rolled one nipple between his fingers before filling his palm with the weight of my breast. Want heated my core as it softened, plumping for him. He trailed his fingers up the inside of my thigh. When he traced my seam, I cried out again. He teased and circled my sensitive bundle of nerves, driving me close to the edge, only to stop.

When his fingers dipped between my folds, I gasped at the burst of sensations. Arching into him as he teased my clit then dipped his finger inside, I panted, hypersensitive to his every touch. He increased the tempo, and I thrust my hips to meet him.

"Please." I needed more of him.

His fingers played me, and I thrashed, trembling from his touch. Passion built between us until I thought I couldn't take much more. My climax was so close. The hard press of him so near my entrance tormented me. I needed him to enter me, desperate for fullness.

My fingers trailed over his skin, loving the leashed strength that jumped and bulged from his muscles at my touch. A wicked thought urged me to turn the tables. Fair play and all that, since he wasn't filling me as I wanted. I wrapped my fingers around his thick length. His body stilled. I pumped my hand in a slow caress. A deep moan reverberated from his chest, vibrating against my skin before escaping his lips.

Our gazes clashed and held. Want pulsed in his dilated pupils. Heat exploded in my core from the intensity of his desire for me, slicking the way for his entry. I arched my back, desperate for him to fill me.

He grabbed his wallet and withdrew a condom. As he rolled it on, I teetered there, wanting to curse him for bringing me to the brink of release before easing off. Then he aligned his hard length with my entrance before he pushed inside and thrust deeply. I arched my back higher to meet him as feverish nerve impulses detonated from the contact. Our lips clashed together in a drugging kiss. My head swam from the sensations cresting inside. It was too much, yet not enough.

With each powerful penetration, I clung to him, his corded muscles shifting beneath my hands. He increased the pace, then his hand slipped between us, dipping between my folds and tracing gentle circles on my clit. I exploded, my climax stealing my breath and clenching like a vise around him. With a roar, he followed.

I could feel the echo of his heart pounding against mine as we lay together, catching our breath. What had happened between us shook me to my core. *What was that?* I'd never experienced such bliss with a man before him. Warmth spread through me, and I glanced at his chiseled features.

A slow smile curved his firm lips before he pressed a kiss to mine. When he shifted to his side, I mourned the loss of him. He rolled off the bed and pulled me to my feet. As he disposed of the condom, I cleaned up and slipped into a pair of panties. We climbed back into bed, and he tucked me against his side.

I lay in his arms, content, and my eyelids grew heavy. I'd let my guard down with him and had been rewarded well. Trust wasn't something I gave lightly. Not anymore. The realization that I trusted him completely was nothing short of a miracle.

With that revelation, I laid my palm over his heart and used his chest as a pillow, enjoying just being with him in the moment.

———

Kylian

Gia lay sprawled across my body, her cheek on my chest. I traced circles over the intricate daisy tattoo on the silky skin of her inner wrist while the gentle rocking of the boat lured us toward sleep. Our legs were tangled together, and her toes curled from my touch.

"For the record, Melanie means nothing to me, and you never have to worry about me cheating." My gut clenched at the confession. I didn't like sharing it, but she deserved to know. When she'd confronted me about Melanie, the hurt in her eyes hadn't escaped my notice. "I grew up watching my father break my mother's heart. The divorce was a long time coming but no less brutal. It shattered my mom. I would never do that to a person."

She lifted her head from my chest and pushed higher so we were eye to eye. Then her lips were on mine, soft and inviting. All it took with her was one touch, and my body came alive. I was there for it.

I tugged her panties off then flipped her so she was underneath me. Her legs wrapped around my waist. I pressed against the heat of her entrance and had just enough sense to reach for my wallet. She laughed as I fumbled for a condom. Once it was on, I slid inside to the addictive sound of her moan.

Much later, we took turns in the bathroom, and I disposed of the condom. Then I tucked her against my side as I climbed back into bed. I wanted more time with her. With so many responsibilities for school, football, and my mom, sharing something we both loved was something I could give Gia. It was a part of me, and from how she'd talked about her uncle, it was also important to her. "We have a home game in two weeks. Do you want to go? Ares's mom and nephew will be there. You could sit with them."

"Really?" She pushed herself up onto an elbow and grinned at me. "Okay. I would love to."

"I'll leave the SUV with you and catch a ride with my roommates. I'll text you a picture of where your seat will be."

She worried her lip with her teeth, her gorgeous blue eyes sparkling with excitement before she settled back into my arms.

The night had started terribly, but being there with Gia… something had clicked. It felt like where we were supposed to be, at least for the time being. Falling asleep with her in my arms was the most natural thing I'd ever done.

CHAPTER SIXTEEN

GIA

Kylian threaded his fingers through mine as we entered his mom's apartment. He deposited the takeout bags on the coffee table. The smells of orange chicken, fried rice, and spring rolls filled the small living room.

"Hi, Evalyn." I moved out from behind Kylian and smiled. "I'll grab some drinks if that's okay?"

"Of course." She pulled the throw covering her legs higher. "And thank you both for picking up food. I had a craving, and I've learned to give in to them, since my appetite isn't always great."

I hurried into the kitchen then leaned against the counter. Elbows on the cool surface, I rested my head in my hands. What we were doing was crazy, and I wasn't sure how I felt about the lies.

"Hey." Kylian's hand rested on the small of my back. "Are you okay?"

"Yeah." I straightened and shifted to face him. "I didn't expect to see her looking so weak today."

I didn't know why. He'd prepared me from the start of our deal. It was probably because Evalyn Wilder had a big personality, like her son, and seeing her even remotely diminished was a shock.

"That's why what we're doing is a good idea. Trust me. She'll be happy."

I saw what he didn't say in his eyes—that it was all he wanted, to make his mom happy and eliminate any lingering worries.

"Okay, I'm all right."

After opening a cabinet, I got three glasses and filled them with water. Kylian took two, and I brought mine and followed him back to the living room. I took a deep breath and pasted on a smile that I hoped looked relaxed.

Kylian set the glasses on the coffee table then pulled me to his side. "Mom, we have some news."

It looked like we were doing it before dinner. I braced myself for the role I would have to play.

Tired deep-blue eyes rose. "Oh?" The ghost of a smile curved her pale lips.

Kylian's hand squeezed my hip, and I leaned into him, trying to help him sell us as a happy couple.

"We got engaged."

Her eyes widened, a spark of something that looked suspiciously like hope lightening them. I held my hand out to her, showing off the ring. It seemed like the right thing to do. I followed it with a soft laugh. "He surprised me." Turning in his arms a little, I gazed at him like I was in love. "Of course, I said yes."

"This is wonderful news." Evalyn stood on shaky legs, and Kylian immediately released me to help her. "I'm thrilled." She wrapped her arms around her son, the lines around her mouth fading as she hugged him.

I got it in that moment. Evalyn looked as if a hundred pounds had been lifted from her shoulders. Then she waved for me to join them. Kylian opened one of his arms, and he and Evalyn both embraced me tight.

"I'm so happy. You have no idea. And, Gia"—she pressed a chilled hand to my cheek—"I've always wanted to have a daughter. I couldn't have hoped for a lovelier one than you. Welcome to our family."

Tears filled my eyes, and my heart cracked in two. If only it were real. I would have loved having her as a mother-in-law. I inhaled slowly as a tear broke through my lashes and rolled down my cheek. I couldn't look at Kylian, preferring to think he hadn't seen, though I could feel him looking at me. "Thank you. I'm honored to be a part of your family." I gently pressed my hand over the back of hers.

Kylian caught my gaze, and he mouthed, *Thank you*, over his mom's head. I nodded, the enormousness of what we were doing, of what he was giving to her, settling in. I could do my part for both of them. And if my heart got broken when she passed away and Kylian and I parted ways, so be it. The scariest part was I was no longer pretending.

CHAPTER SEVENTEEN

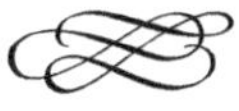

KYLIAN

I sat in the back row of my finance class, with Liam and Ares on either side of me, while the professor droned on about risk management. I was counting down the minutes for class to end so I could talk to them without the press of people all around us. I toyed with my pen, my laptop open to maintain the appearance of taking notes, but the class was a cakewalk for Ares and me. Liam struggled a little with it. I made a mental note to check in and see how he was doing later.

When we finally filed out of our last, packed class for the day, I took advantage of the buzz of conversation around us. On our walk through campus to football practice, I told them what was happening. It was time, and I needed them onboard.

"Gia and I had dinner with my mom last night."

"How's Evalyn?" Ares asked, and Liam glanced at me.

"She's tired and looked like she was in pain. But once we shared our news, all that went away. It was like watching a weight lift off her shoulders."

"What news?" Liam's brows furrowed.

"Gia and I told her we're engaged."

"What the fuck are you talking about? You just met the girl."

Liam reared back, jostling our teammate, one of the defensive ends, who was taking up maximum space on his other side as we crossed the quad. He was in a boisterous conversation with whoever was on his far side, so I didn't worry overmuch that we might be overheard.

"Isn't it a little early to get engaged?" Ares took a calmer approach to the same response.

"Sure. If it were real." I filled them in on how Gia and I met, the contract, and why the fake engagement helped me with my parents in vastly different ways.

"So Evalyn was happy about the news? She believed you?" Ares dropped his voice.

A genuine smile curved my mouth for the first time that day. "Mom likes Gia a lot. So, yeah. She believed us. I don't know if it was the ring or how real it seemed between us, but she was thrilled, and the relief when she sagged into me was unreal. It had bothered her."

"What? That you hadn't settled down?"

"Yeah. She wished I would find the girl I wanted to marry. She worried I wouldn't before she passed, especially given the limited time the doc had originally said she had left."

"What do you mean originally?" Ares's gaze sharpened, and I read the hope swirling in his topaz eyes.

"We don't know. Hopefully, that'll change with the new treatment. If we're lucky, she'll keep responding, but it's not a guarantee."

With that, we fell silent. The reality of what Mom faced—and what I would face in the wake of her passing—was depressing.

I felt off for the rest of the walk to practice, despite letting my friends in on what was going on in my life. It wasn't until I was on the field, with the football in my hand, that some normalcy crept in. That was where I thrived. It always had been, and I knew without a doubt that football was the right career for me—if and when I entered the draft. The only problem was anything could happen—an injury or any number of things.

Ares, Liam, and the other receivers lined up, ready to run drills with me. Calvin, the backup quarterback, palmed a football as the second string prepared to do the same with him.

"Don't get too comfortable, QB1." Calvin's grin was sly. He was an antagonistic fucker. "You can't hold onto the starting position all year. As soon as you screw up, I'll be on the field, securing the spot."

I laughed. "You can try." It wasn't the way I should've responded. I needed to be a leader and teach him to read plays better. He sucked at spotting blitzes. If he weren't such an evil asshole, I would've spent time with him and taught him. Instead, I regularly watched film with the third-string QB, a freshman. He had the right attitude, and I firmly believed he would take over my position next year. I did other things for him, like making sure the coach knew we watched film together, and he sometimes joined Ares, Liam, and me on our morning runs.

But I didn't need to focus on that problem, or the bullshit Calvin would spew every chance he got. I could read him like a book. Something was eating at him. He was at his worst during those times. I had no idea how his cousin Maverick dealt with him, let alone defended him. I must be missing something about Calvin because Mav, aside from fighting Liam that one time, was a good guy.

I pushed everything from my mind as the quarterback coach called plays, tossing me the ball so I could execute them. While I did drills, everything felt right with my world. I just hoped it would stay that way.

CHAPTER EIGHTEEN

GIA

I cracked an eyelid open and peered at the clock. I had to blink a few times and shove my hair out of my face before I could read the time. Eight in the morning. Kylian had left a half hour ago and told me to stay, that he would drive me back to the boat after his class. I stretched, luxuriating in his bed with the addictive scent of him all around me. Two weeks had passed since the reporters had followed me and the dinner with his mom when we'd told her we were engaged. Warmth filled me at the memory of how happy she'd been. What Kylian was doing—the fake engagement—it was so worth it to see the joy shining in her eyes.

Last night, we'd stayed at his place. The time Kylian and I spent on the boat wasn't enough, and we often alternated between there and the condo. If it worked with his schedule, we went on the boat, which usually ended up being a few times a week and after we had dinner with his mom. It'd become a pattern, and I wasn't sorry about it. I tried not to read too much into how easy things were between us, but it was hard not to.

Another half hour passed before I dragged myself from bed,

showered, and ventured into the condo's kitchen. I ran my hand over the gorgeous, lightly veined white quartz countertop. I'd been dreaming about cooking in there. It was my chance. I suppressed a squeal.

The condo was quiet, and I wasn't sure if Kylian's roommates were sleeping or in class. It was hard to believe that three guys lived there, given how clean everything was. I expected the kitchen to be a pigsty with used dishes in the sink. I opened the dishwasher and found a mess of dirty plates. I guessed that was the extent of their being slobs—they'd forgotten to run it the night before. A grin curved my mouth. I could work with that. After cooking breakfast, I would just start the load for them with my dishes inside. No one would know I'd even ventured in there or eaten their food. Not that it was a big deal, since Kylian said I could help myself to anything I wanted, and that had been in front of Ares and Liam. Neither of them had protested.

I pulled out eggs, veggies, a package of shredded cheddar cheese, and a loaf of whole wheat bread. I got to work chopping the vegetables then heard the shower turn on in one of the bedrooms. A door closed, and another opened. Liam appeared. Ares must be the one in the shower, then. I bent my head and continued my task while he helped himself to a cup of coffee.

I risked a glance when he sat across from me on one of the island chairs. I wasn't sure what to make of Liam. I was comfortable around Ares—I related to his sincerity and the sadness that sometimes swam in his eyes—but Liam seemed like more of a player.

He took a sip of coffee before setting it down. "You cook?"

Heat flooded my cheeks. The kitchen was my happy place, but I wasn't sure I was genuinely welcome in their domain. "Yeah, did you want anything?"

He snorted. "Turn down food? That's not gonna happen here. If you're offering, I'm eating."

"Me too!" Ares shouted from somewhere near his room before appearing beside the island, hope on his gorgeous face.

The tension melted from my shoulders, and another spark of excitement added speed to my knife skills. With two skillets heating on the burner, I beat the eggs to make omelets. Bubbles rolled to the surface in a pot of water I'd set to boil, and I carefully placed a few eggs in before setting a timer for a soft boil.

When the omelets were ready, I slid them onto two plates. Bread went into the toaster, and I snagged two ripe avocados.

Ares and Liam chatted in the background, making it impossible not to listen. A phone buzzed, vibrating on the counter as I turned for the shredded cheddar. I sprinkled a little on the omelets then set the plates before the guys.

"Oh, wow. Gia"—Ares shoveled another bite in his mouth—"this is amazing."

"Thanks." I grinned then got to work on the soft-boiled eggs. When they were ready, I peeled and sliced them in half. The toast was done. Avocado went on a few pieces, then the egg halves, and finally, I sprinkled seasoning and pine nuts over the top. I took one for myself and left the other two for the guys if they wanted more.

"Are you eating these?" Liam paused, his hand halfway to the plate of avocado toast.

"No"—I lifted my toast—"I have some already. That's for you guys if you want it." I knew they needed to consume a lot of protein. More eggs wouldn't be turned down.

"You're an angel," Liam moaned around a bite.

I froze at the term of endearment. Even innocently said, it made the blood drain from my face, and my food-holding hand trembled.

"Are you okay?" Ares zeroed in on my reaction.

"Oh, um. Yeah, I just don't like that term of endearment."

"My bad." Liam never looked up. His eyes closed in bliss as he finished the last bit of toast.

Ares smacked him in the shoulder.

"What? I saved you a piece," Liam groused.

Ares rolled his eyes, giving up and looking back at me. "Sure, you're all right?"

"Yeah, I am." I took a deep breath and tried to brush aside the unwanted memories that the term of endearment brought. It was what Dayton liked to call me. It had become more of a curse than anything and set my teeth on edge if I heard it about me.

But that was then. I was safe. Two giant ballers who I was starting to care about were sitting opposite me, and the building had a doorman. With that reminder, I relaxed again, knowing Liam hadn't meant anything by it. He was pretty oblivious with food in front of him.

"Anytime you feel like cooking, we're down for it. This is amazing." Liam licked his fingers before gulping coffee.

"It was." Ares grinned before stacking our plates and taking them to the sink, where he rinsed them then put them in the dishwasher. "Thanks, Gia."

Liam's phone vibrated with a call, and his easygoing mood vanished. His brows pulled down, and his lips pressed into a tight line. "Fuck."

Ares rounded the counter and glanced at his phone. "Brittany again?"

"That girl can't take a hint."

"I told you not to sleep with her. She has professional-athlete-wife goals, and you're her latest target. You know how long it took Craig to shake her?"

Liam continued to frown, shifting the glare he'd given his phone to Ares.

"A year and a half. It wasn't until he graduated and went into the NHL that she gave up. And that was just because he's in another state."

I reached for the phone. "Do you mind?" I grinned, wanting

to help and loving that I could mess with a stalker from a safe distance, where it wouldn't come back on me.

Liam shrugged. "Go ahead. Just don't tell her I'm here."

I pressed the button to accept the call. "Hello?"

"Who's this?" Brittany's high-pitched voice rose at the end. "I'm looking for Liam." She didn't even wait for a name.

"He's in the shower. Hold on a sec. We only just woke up." I semi-muffled the phone. "Hon, you have a call." I looked at him expectantly.

Lips twitching at the corners, he stood and moved to the other side of the room before saying, "Don't care. Get your fine ass in here. I'm not done with you."

I played along. "Babe, I'm so tired. You kept me up most of the night. Let's go to breakfast first. We can have a repeat after classes."

Liam slapped his hand over his mouth, muffling his laughter.

I waited another second before fumbling with the phone like I was picking it back up. "Hey, sorry. He's busy. I'll let him know you called." I hung up and put down his phone.

"Holy fuck." Ares grinned. "If I ever get a stalker, I want you on my team too."

Liam joined us back at the island, slapping Ares on the shoulder. "You had one last year."

"Dawn. Wow, I forgot about her."

"She gave up on you because you never date and showed zero interest in her because, as you claimed, you were too busy."

Ares shrugged. "Speaking of busy, we have class in fifteen minutes. Are you gonna be around after, Gia?"

"Kylian's driving me back to the pier after he's done with class, so probably not."

"This has been a fantastic morning." Liam grinned. "I hope to see you around a lot more. Later, Gia."

"I agree." Ares smiled before picking up his backpack and

following Liam out the door. "You're good for Kyl. It's nice having you around."

I couldn't stop smiling, even after they left. What they'd said meant a lot, even if my relationship with Kylian had an expiration date. I could still enjoy my time with him and the guys while it lasted.

CHAPTER NINETEEN

GIA

It was a beautiful Saturday afternoon, if a little too hot, as I walked into Fall Lake University's stadium. The afternoon sun blazed high in the sky, and the crowd pressed around me. The air buzzed with excitement, and not even the slightest hint of fear crept in as I stood among the hyped football fans. I didn't even care that it was televised because my ex hated football. He wouldn't be caught dead watching a game. I was perfectly safe and loving every moment of the experience.

It was my first in-person game. A pang of longing for my uncle swept through me, there and gone in a second. He would have loved this—going to Kylian's game, cheering in the stands with the rest of the crowd. Even though he wasn't with me, I felt him in our shared love for the sport.

The smell of popcorn and fried food from the concession stands permeated the air. Blue and silver filled the stands, and I lost count of the sheer volume of girls wearing players' jersey numbers on their shirts or painted on their cheeks.

I wore an older jersey of Kylian's, cinched at my waist with a knot. It was huge, but I couldn't pass up the chance to wear it when he'd offered. Besides, I was supposed to be his fiancée, so it made sense that I would be present. Ares and Liam had been just as vocal as Kylian about me going to the game. It helped me feel as if I was there to support them.

I followed the directions from Kylian's last text and looked for the people in the picture he'd also sent, one of a pretty woman and young boy who were Ares's mom and nephew. The stands on the side where I stood were filled with blue and silver, the university colors.

It wasn't long before I spotted a woman who resembled Ares. She had shoulder-length dark-blond hair, and when she turned toward me as I made my way down the aisle to the empty seat next to her, I met her topaz eyes. The boy, who had to be around thirteen or fourteen, had the same eyes but dark-brown hair. They both wore Ares's jersey number.

"Hi." I smiled at them as I sat. "I'm Gia."

"Hey, Gia. I'm Julie, Ares's mom, and this is my grandson, Preston."

I waved to him and got a quick acknowledgment, then his focus turned to the corner where the footballers would make their entrance.

I leaned close to Julie to be heard over the people around us. "Thanks for saving me a seat."

"Of course." Julie squeezed my hand then released it. Sadness clung to the edges of her eyes, as it did with Ares. It was impossible not to notice, but it didn't feel like my place to ask if everything was okay.

Preston jumped to his feet, a roar leaving his lips as the jumbotron zeroed in on the corner where a swarm of reporters and commentators waited. Fans joined him in a frenzy of blue towels whirling overhead. Ear-piercing screams filled the air as the Fall Lake Ballers ran onto the field. Fireworks shot from the top of the stadium, and everyone in the crowd went crazy. The stands shook like an earthquake struck them from people jumping up and down.

Nothing matched the thunderous excitement of our team taking the field. After the coin toss, I perched on the edge of my seat, along with everyone else, and the teams lined up against each other at the start of the game.

The ball snapped into Kylian's hands, and he backed into the pocket, scanning the field. Liam took off like a shot. Kylian locked on him and launched the ball. It soared in the air then fell into Liam's hand without him breaking stride. Ares followed, delivering a crucial block that could've taken Liam down. We gained twenty yards.

The ball was tossed to a ref, and they lined up, ready to go again. Play after play kept me on pins and needles. They got to work, each play gaining yards and first downs until they were in the end zone. I held my breath as Kylian handed the ball off to Ares, and he plowed through the defensive line and into the end zone—we were on the board. They had killer instincts, especially Kylian. The guys were thrilling to watch.

I jumped up and down, receiving a hug from Julie and a high five from Preston. I was hooked, and nothing could tear me away from the thrilling atmosphere of an in-person game. Their offense and defense were equally matched. The offense drove the ball relentlessly, and our defense held the other team for very few first downs and only one touchdown. We had three.

The game was mesmerizing, and when halftime neared, Julie, Preston, and I gushed over what'd happened. Then the players returned, and something shifted in the stand as Fall Lake U's three top players took the field along with the rest of their teammates. Something about them was special, especially Kylian. He did things few quarterbacks in the NFL did—outrun, sidearm throw, break for tackles, and still read the field in a split second, delivering the ball into his teammates' hands like he wasn't about to go down.

Fall Lake U dominated, pulling out a massive win. The stands erupted at the end of the game, and I shouted right along with them. A sense of awe filled me from watching the sheer athleticism Kylian displayed. The team was fantastic, but I mostly had eyes on those three. The difference between experiencing a game in person and watching a televised one narrowed to the energy. After that experience, I wanted to go to all Kylian's games.

I t was late by the time I got back to the condo with Kylian and his roommates. We'd gone out to dinner with Ares's mom and nephew. By the time we got back, I was exhausted. I'd slept over so many times, I didn't bother asking if he cared and said good night, leaving the guys to talk in the kitchen as I fell into Kylian's bed.

Things between us were good, and it scared me a little. I kept waiting for the other shoe to drop, and as I drifted on the edge of sleep, the fear—and past trauma—that I'd been ignoring and holding at bay for weeks rose to the surface. They only worsened as I sank deeper into unconsciousness.

Somewhere in the condo, a door shut, and the soft click echoed in my soul. I tossed and turned in bed, the covers tangling around my legs as they fought to escape—seeking any amount of freedom. It wasn't meant to be. I knew what was coming and was powerless to stop it as I sank into the nightmare. No matter how hard I sought the light, my eyelids remained shut.

Footsteps padded across the marble entryway. Each caused my heart rate to accelerate. The phantom hand of terror squeezed around my neck. Dayton called that morning and told me to meet him at the country club, where he was having lunch with some bigwigs like himself. I was to go and be the trophy on his arm that he'd trained me to be. I couldn't do it and silently rebelled at his demand, so I would pay the price.

The fine hairs on my arms and the back of my neck stood as if an electrical storm raged. But it wasn't the weather. It was my impending doom. I should have gone, smiled and nodded, done what he'd wanted. But when I'd woken that morning, grief from my uncle's passing had kept me prisoner and easy prey for a man like Dayton—I should have read the danger signs. I couldn't pretend things would get better, that Dayton was under a lot of stress and pressure. He was a monster. I'd seen the truth of it one too many times—and without blinders.

"You embarrassed me." His voice was smooth, low, and controlled—the worst version of his moods.

I didn't turn around. Large hands encircled my arms in a too-firm grip. I repressed a shiver, clearing my voice instead. "I wasn't feeling well and fell asleep."

"You should have set an alarm." He leaned in, trailing his nose along the curve of my neck, inhaling my scent. "There's no excuse for what you did."

I choked down the retort on the tip of my tongue. It would only make things worse. "I'm sorry. I think I had a fever. It wouldn't have been good to get your associates sick... or you." He could rot in hell for all I cared.

The room spun too fast, and I landed on the kitchen floor with a thud. Dayton loomed over me after tossing me like I weighed nothing. I sucked air in and forced it out, trying to control the cloying fear that threatened to take over. He took a step forward. I gritted my teeth, planted my hands on the floor for leverage, and kicked his leg with all my might.

A grunt passed his lips, and triumph urged me to try again. I wouldn't go down without a fight. Not anymore. I aimed for his knee and kicked, but his meaty hand wrapped around my ankle and squeezed before he yanked me closer.

All thoughts fled, and I became a fury of motion, slapping, hitting, scratching, and punching. The world tunneled, and I reacted. I lost time. It was always like that—blind panic fueled with the instinct to fight.

When he straddled me, his substantial weight stealing my breath, I prayed for unconsciousness. The first hit came—opened palm to the face. My head whipped to the side. Blood filled my mouth. Pain followed.

He leaned close, his hand closing around my throat. Pressure restricted my oxygen, and I bucked, trying to dislodge him, but he was too big and heavy.

"You brought this on yourself." Cold fury danced like an out-of-control flame in his eyes. "I'm going to spend tonight teaching you about obedience." He stood and dragged me to my feet by my neck. Fingers twisted in my hair, and he jerked my head back, his mouth crushing mine in a brutal kiss. "I own you, Angel. Body and soul. And I will ensure that you never forget it after tonight."

"Go to hell." I spat in his face.

The sight of splattered saliva and blood dotting his skin was short-lived when he grabbed my hand and slammed it and my wrist along the corner of the counter. Bones snapped, and I screamed.

"Gia!"

I gasped, cradling my wrist to my chest. My body shook, and I blinked in confusion as my surroundings slowly came into focus. There was no pain. The scent of danger and the familiar taste of fear vanished. My bloodcurdling scream died as a door opened, slamming against the wall, and light flooded the space.

Gentle hands pulled me to a firm, warm chest. I struggled to separate the horror of the too-real nightmare from the present. But I would know the body pressed against mine anywhere. In Kylian's arms, a measure of safety penetrated my fear.

"What's wrong with her?" Concern threaded Ares's question.

I blinked again, taking note of Ares and Liam, both without shirts and in their boxer briefs, standing in the doorway with pale faces and identical expressions of shock and distress. Heat flooded my cheeks, and I clung to Kylian, thankful for the shelter of his embrace.

"It was a nightmare," I croaked, voice partially muffled by his bicep.

"That didn't sound like a nightmare." Ares's brows furrowed. "Are you sure you're okay? Liam and I can kick Kylian's ass if he did anything."

"Get the fuck out." Kylian's words held no heat as he rubbed soothing circles on my back.

"Right." Liam cleared his throat. "The offer stands, Gia. Just say the word, and we'll pound Kylian into the turf." A flash of humor chased some of the worry from his green eyes. "Or we'll make sure the O-line lets through the opposing team's defensive tackle—every play."

A subdued laugh left my lips, and I sagged into Kylian, letting him take my weight. I appreciated them even more. "Thanks, guys. But I promise I'm okay. It was just a freakishly real nightmare. I have to stop watching horror movies because they clearly affect me."

Liam snorted, rapped his knuckles on the doorframe, and pivoted. "I'm out. Glad you're okay, G."

Ares stood there another moment, locked in a stare with Kylian. Whatever silent conversation took place between the two must've finally reassured him because he nodded, grabbed the doorknob, and shut the door quietly behind him.

A few seconds passed, and the nightmare lost its grip on me, but I didn't move from Kylian's arms. He made me feel safe, a phenomenon I didn't take for granted.

"Want to talk about it?" His words were soft and soothing.

"I-I..." My throat locked, and I shivered. I wanted to tell him so badly. "No." I couldn't. Not then. I didn't want to relive it or see pity in his beautiful eyes. "It's... nothing. I'm just embarrassed."

"Don't be. There's no reason for that. Ares had some wicked nightmares a few years ago, and Liam sleepwalks. I should have told you about it in case you ever got up during the night and thought he was a zombie with the weird, vacant look on his face."

I laughed. "That's good to know. I'll avoid waking him if I run into him in that state."

"You know you're safe here, right? I won't let anything… or anyone hurt you."

"Yeah, I do. Thank you." I swiped a tear from my cheek with the tip of my finger, my heart cracking enough for him to slip all the way in.

CHAPTER TWENTY

GIA

Three Weeks Later

It was criminally early, the sun barely cresting the horizon to stream through the small porthole. Heat blanketed my back from Kylian's large body spooning mine. I eased from beneath his heavy arm. Once free, I stretched then got out of bed. It was a new day, and I braced myself against my conflicting emotions. I already feared I was falling for him too hard and too fast. Just the hint of my out-of-control feelings was enough to douse the flame pooling low in my stomach with the need for round three.

I'd slipped into a pair of panties last night, but that was it. My fingers hooked the white dress shirt he'd tossed on the floor after he'd worn it on the flight to his away game the previous day. I pushed my arms into it, working a few buttons through their holes to keep it mostly closed.

It would have been nice to go to the game, but I'd attended all his home games since my first, several weeks ago. It'd become a habit to sit with Ares's mom and nephew, which was fun. I enjoyed their company. When Kylian and I were alone hours later, we would talk about the plays. Getting that part of my life back was a gift I would always be grateful to him for.

After we'd gotten ready for bed, he'd set his alarm for nine to make his ten-o'clock class. I didn't want to wake him, since he had about an hour before he had to get up. I made coffee to drink on the deck in the morning sun. I headed up the stairs to unlock the door to the cabin. It opened easily.

It wasn't until I was on the deck that the sound of hushed voices too close to where I stood registered. My head whipped up, and my gaze jumped around until it landed on a man and woman a few feet from where I stood. I froze when I took in the man in the business suit. He was an older version of Kylian. A woman not too much older than me stood by his side. Heat rushed to my face as I realized what I was, and wasn't, wearing in front of Kylian's father as he studied me. He did not look amused.

"Ahh, one second." A quick pivot, and I rushed down the stairs.

I deposited the mug of coffee on the counter, splashing hot liquid over the rim in my haste to get to the primary bedroom. I yanked the pillow from beneath Kylian's head, and he came instantly awake.

"You've got to stop doing that," he growled then reached for me.

I'd already moved back in anticipation. "Your father is on the deck."

"Fuck." He launched himself from the bed and shoved his legs into his dress pants. He zipped and buttoned them, not bothering with a shirt.

Well, I'm wearing it, so what could he do?

He was through the galley and on the stairs before I could

find yesterday's shirt—mine, not his. When I managed to get dressed, I headed for the deck but stopped near the stairs when I heard Kylian's and his father's heated voices volleying back and forth. Unsure what to do, I stayed rooted to the spot and eavesdropped shamelessly.

"Impossible. I'm already engaged to Gia," Kylian growled.

"Absolutely not," his father snapped. "I already promised Honeycutt that you'll marry his daughter. He says she has her sights set on an NFL quarterback, and you're the one she wants."

"I don't care if her daddy thinks he can get her anything she wants, including me. I've already chosen my path, and Melanie Honeycutt isn't on it."

"You're making a big mistake, son. She would be the perfect wife. A true chameleon and able to fit into any social event you're required to attend. But if you want to pass up the best thing that could happen to you... If you don't want to marry the Honeycutt girl and live in the lap of luxury"—his father's deep voice was resolute and threatening—"you can marry the little slut listening in the cabin and risk whatever dirt that I find in her past tarnishing your life. And let's not forget about what your mother needs, hmm?"

Slut? I jumped back. *Can he see me? What should I do? Pretend I wasn't listening, or not deny anything and go up there, defend myself, and find out what Kylian wants to do?*

The click of stilettos crossed the deck. Hatred for his father chased away the momentary shock of what he'd called me. When no more footfalls sounded, I knew Mr. Wilder and his young wife had left.

The second option won as an invisible thread pulled me to Kylian, and I scaled the stairs. He stood with a white-knuckled grip on the stern railing, looking over the water, his back to the dock. Mirroring his pose, I curled my fingers around the metal, not turning toward him until he moved. Our gazes locked and held, and I gasped at the torment swimming through his smoky-blue eyes. My lungs squeezed, and an ache thrummed in my chest. It was an odd feeling to see him like that—vulnerable.

"Ignore what my dad said about you. He's an ass."

"It's forgotten." Sort of. Okay, it wasn't. I would forever hold that against his father. It was too great an insult to call me a slut when he knew nothing about me.

Kylian's hand settled on my hip. When his other arm wrapped around me and pulled me against his solid chest, I briefly shut my eyes and savored the moment. It couldn't last, no matter how much I liked being in his arms or how safe he made me feel.

I took a deep breath then said what needed to be vocalized. I knew other things were at stake from how affected he'd seemed. "We can dissolve our agreement. No harm. No foul. Just pretend that there wasn't one."

"Gia, my dad will not win this game he's playing." He notched my chin up so we were looking at each other again.

Based on the aftereffects of their encounter swimming in his eyes, I wasn't so sure.

"We're not giving him the satisfaction of bowing out early. That was his first strike. There will be more, but we're in this together with something to gain."

I curled my arms around his neck, wanting to believe him despite the odds I sensed were stacked against us. I couldn't imagine a father doing that to his son. I didn't have a father figure, except for my uncle, and he never would have done anything to hurt or use me. It was unfathomable. Pushing onto my toes, I tugged on Kylian's neck until he lowered his face. And I brushed my lips against his in a gentle caress.

None of that was part of our contract, but the more time I spent with him, the more my walls crumbled. Thoughts fled as he took control of the kiss and swept his tongue past my parted lips to tangle with mine. My head spun, and I squeezed my thighs against the throbbing caused by his simple touch.

He nipped my bottom lip then eased the sting with a swipe of his tongue. I moaned, melting against him. Then his hands cupped my bottom, and he lifted me, my legs automatically wrapping around him. Short, silky strands of hair at the back of his neck met my fingers, and I toyed with them. I wanted to feel all of him. Clothes were an unwanted barrier.

He broke the kiss, pressing his forehead against mine. We took a minute to catch our breath, and as our surroundings came back into focus, surprise danced over my bare arms despite the September heat.

I wanted to strip him and myself bare out in the open. Relinquishing the tight hold with my legs, I slid them down his body until my feet were firmly planted on the deck. Then I rested my palms against his chest and slid my fingers to his broad shoulders, holding on to the tense muscle.

"I…" *What?* I was so consumed by how he made me feel that I'd lost sight of our surroundings. That wasn't smart. On the heels of that thought, the fine hairs on the back of my neck rose with the sensation of being watched, and a jolt of fear surged through me. My muscles locked down as I did a visual sweep, assuring myself my ex wasn't lurking in the shadows somewhere.

"Let's take this below deck."

The deep timbre of his voice, hoarse with desire, sent an entirely different kind of tingle dancing over my body, chasing most of my worries aside. I glanced around again, quickly, ever mindful of photographers or someone much worse. When I didn't see anyone, the feeling passed. I was being ridiculous. I'd been careful and wouldn't stop being cautious.

With a slow smile, I gave into my need for him that was impossible to deny. "What are you waiting for?"

He whirled and picked me up again. I clutched him tighter, laughter and a sense of freedom filling me. He carried me down the stairs, pausing to close and latch the door behind us.

As we tumbled into bed, I welcomed his weight, giving myself over to the passion only he could give me.

CHAPTER TWENTY-ONE

KYLIAN

I was furious Dad had stopped by the boat when he'd learned from Honeycutt that I'd been avoiding Melanie's calls. I'd made no promises where she was concerned, and I resented what he was attempting. But for the time, all I could do about him insulting Gia was damage control.

After a quick shower and change into clothes I kept on the boat, I left Gia, who was sexy as hell and fast asleep. I had enough time to call for a ride, get to my condo, grab my laptop, and go to class. I didn't like leaving her without a vehicle, and I tried to provide mine whenever possible. On the ride, I went through messages and emails, handling what I could until the driver pulled up along the curb in front of my building.

"Sir." The doorman stopped me. "Your father left strict instructions to let you know the locks are being changed and the penthouse is no longer available to you." George wiped a shaky hand along his forehead, pushing thinning brown hair to the side.

It was bullshit, but he didn't know that. I weighed my options. Both Ares and Liam were in class and wouldn't be any help. I could push my way past the doorman because my dad couldn't change the locks or do anything to my condo. If he wanted to, he could make things very difficult for my roommates and me, since he'd bought the place before I had legal access to the trust from my grandfather. But I'd been paying the mortgage ever since I had access to the money. The ownership was supposed to change when I gained access to the trust, but I'd thought better of outright buying the condo—which had been the original plan—when Mom's bills started rolling in. I'd taken over the payments, with my roommates contributing rent, but hadn't bothered to refinance and transfer everything into my name.

I glanced at George's immaculate suit and how tightly he clasped his hands. "My father is wrong in this." I smiled to remove any perceived reprimand. It wasn't George's fight, and I could tell how much he hated being the bearer of this news. I could've gone in through the garage if I'd had my keycard. I didn't. It was sitting in my SUV, which I'd left for Gia's use. *Is Dad having me followed?* If so—and I wouldn't put it past him—he would've been aware that I didn't have my SUV and maybe the ability to access the garage.

I nodded at George, careful to keep my frustration from my voice. "I have class. Afterward, I'll contact the office to update you and anyone else who needs to know that my dad can't change the locks."

It wouldn't take much—a simple phone call from my lawyer to the building manager, which I would make immediately. It might take some time to update the staff, though. I left, since there was nothing more to do unless I wanted to waste time I didn't have. Instead, I walked to class without my laptop. I had friends who could email me notes if needed. It was bright and sunny, already promising to be a warm day, but my thoughts were elsewhere.

My father was formidable, still a paper trail led to the trust and the condo's monthly mortgage and association payments.

That maneuver was just the start of what my dad planned to throw my way. I would have to figure out how to anticipate his game fast.

If he was having me watched and knew Gia was alone, that left her vulnerable. *That's his plan.* Anger tore through me, and I whipped out my phone, opened my Uber app, and ordered a ride. There was one six minutes away. I could skip class for one day.

I used the time spent waiting for my ride to call my lawyer and get her on my condo problem. Even with one thing checked off my list, impatience continued to buzz under my sun-warmed skin.

When the car dropped me off at the harbor, I quickly spotted the dark sedan that my father favored. The marina wasn't busy, so I hurried along the boardwalk and down the pier to my boat.

Water lapped at the sides of tethered vessels, masking any noise I made during my approach. Voices carried over the cries of seagulls and sound of rippling water. I recognized my dad's and paused out of sight from where he stood, towering over Gia.

"I know your type"—condemnation layered Dad's tone—"a gold digger who found the perfect target. Kylian's connected. And when he gets into the NFL, which is a foregone conclusion, your life is set. It's not going to happen. Here." He must have shoved something at her.

I inched forward, taking care not to be spotted. I fought every nerve in my body telling me to go to her defense, to protect her. I forced myself to stay where I was, knowing I needed as much ammo as I could gain by listening and remaining out of sight.

"What's this?"

"A check. Take it," Dad growled. "Then disappear from Kylian's life for good."

"No." Gia's voice was clear, unwavering. "I'm engaged to your son. I don't want your money."

A bitter laugh carried from where they stood, facing one another. I had to see how far he would go, what he might reveal.

"Fine." Dad reached into his suit, withdrew another check, and held it out to Gia. "This should seal the deal."

Gia's arms crossed over her chest, and her chin rose stubbornly. I couldn't stop the grin from pulling at my mouth if I'd tried.

"That won't change anything. Go ahead, keep upping the amount. It won't matter. I don't want your money, and I'm marrying Kylian."

"That's never going to happen."

"Look, Mr. Wilder, I don't know what type of relationship you two have, but I can promise you that once he hears about your attempt to pay me off, he'll be furious." Her head tilted, and I could picture her gorgeous blue eyes narrowed in challenge. "This"—she pointed at the check still in Dad's hand—"is a sure-fire way to sever the relationship you should wish to have with your son. Now, if you don't want me spilling about what you just tried to do, I suggest you stop pressuring him to help you in your political endeavors."

"You're knocked up, aren't you?"

Gia said nothing.

"You manipulated then trapped him. When he wakes from your scam, he'll leave you high and dry. I suggest you take the money now."

"I'm not pregnant. But I do feel sorry for you. You have a wonderful son, and you seem determined to chip away at what you could have."

"Kylian is cut off. He won't be entitled to a dime of the Wilder money. I suggest you take what I offered, since that's the most you'll ever get out of him."

As Gia shook her head, an idea about how I would play his game took life in mine.

"You underestimate your son."

"No, I don't. I see you for who you are, and I won't let you ruin my chances in the election."

"Please go. We have nothing more to discuss."

That was my cue, and I made my way toward them. They turned as one when I climbed aboard.

I met my dad's surprised gaze. "Nice job with the condo." I didn't let on that I'd heard what he'd just tried to do with Gia.

Dad grinned, but it didn't meet his eyes. They remained cold, calculating. "If you like that, you'll love what'll happen with the shithole your mother lives in. And if that doesn't convince you to get on board with the plan, you and your roommates will need to find other accommodations as well."

I shrugged. He wouldn't go that far, not if it might ruin his image, since reporters were well aware of our connection. "I bet Channel 6 will like it too. And so will the Honeycutts when they see it. They'll love hearing that senatorial candidate and business tycoon Danbury Wilder kicked his ex-wife out of her home. Especially when they learn she has cancer."

I stepped closer, enjoying the fury pinching his mouth and bracketing it with deep frown lines. I lowered my voice, delivering the threat with the precision of a dagger. "Stories like that have sticking power. They live on in people's memories and paint a clear picture of what the asshole who's bullying a dying woman is really like. Those headlines won't go away. I promise that someone will continue to feed more to the press." I had no doubt Mom had insulated herself, and probably me as well, from Dad's threats, but that felt damn good to deliver.

Dad's eyes narrowed, and he pointed a finger in my direction. "Meet me at the office in an hour, and we'll discuss your betrayal."

"That's not going to happen. I have class"—that I'd missed—"then practice. And I expect to sleep in my bed tonight."

"Don't you dare threaten me. Tell the girl to find a new place to stay, or your mother will be put out before the news channel gets wind of what happened."

He brushed past me, and I watched as he strode down the pier, got into his car, and drove away. The hatred I'd had for him before grew into something dark and unmanageable. My greatest concern was Mom and making sure he didn't hurt her.

I turned back to Gia and gripped her shoulders. "I can't let him get to Mom first. I need my keys for the SUV."

Her mouth opened, but no words came out. She gave a clipped nod, wrenched her shoulders free, then pulled the keys from her pocket and dropped them into my hand. She turned, her long dark hair fanning as she raced down the stairs. I had to force myself to leave when she disappeared, though all I wanted to do was follow her.

As I hurried off the boat and down the pier, my thoughts warred over not reassuring Gia. I should have made my presence known and gotten between her and my father sooner. But I couldn't focus on that until later. I had to make sure Mom was safe.

CHAPTER TWENTY-TWO

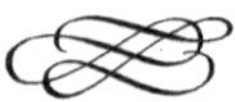

GIA

My hands shook as I pushed my hair away from my face. I paced in a small circle in the boat's primary sleeping cabin while Kylian's Dad's words played in my head. I'd been insulted, accused of intentionally getting pregnant and targeting Kylian for his money—okay, that one hurt because it aligned too closely with the truth. Sort of. It was a mutually beneficial contract, and recently… circumstances had changed our deal.

I never should have let him kiss me.

The encounter with Mr. Wilder had been so full of drama and painful accusations. I hadn't been that emotionally abused since Dayton, another time I would never forget, though I wished I could.

Screw it. I grabbed my purse, raced up the stairs, and slammed the door that separated the lower quarters from the deck. I had to get away and clear my head. The attempted payoff made me feel dirty. I hated when people used money to control and manipulate situations and people to their benefit, and that was exactly what Mr. Wilder had done.

I jogged down the dock, wondering what I should do and

where I could spend the night. I didn't want another run-in with Mr. Wilder, and Kylian wouldn't be there to run interference. I would have time to return and get my things once I had a plan. Fortunately, Kylian had football practice, so he wouldn't be back. I didn't want him to know I was running scared.

Wandering along Chicago's lakefront eased some of the chaos churning in my mind. Navy Pier wasn't far from where Kylian docked his boat. I could see the Ferris wheel spinning, the sun glinting off the metal against the clear blue sky.

I couldn't blame Kylian for putting his mom first. His dad probably wouldn't come back while I was alone. *Right?* He should care for his mom's well-being. I would've too.

I kicked at a pebble and cringed when it bounced off the leg of a woman in front of me. She didn't spare me a glance as she hurried down the sidewalk, weaving through people ahead of her. I didn't want to be alone with my thoughts. When I reached Navy Pier, I turned toward it along with several others. It was loud and teeming with people. One of the three huge dining and entertainment boats that typically parked at the dock was out carrying a lunch crowd.

The pier was busier than usual, with booths and games lining the dock—some kind of event. *A carnival of sorts?* Despite being late afternoon, the lighting from the flashing colors, games, and rides felt eerie.

A hint of mint permeated the air. The abhorrent smell disoriented me, sending a sliver of fear in its wake, and I stumbled, bumping into someone on my left. As I turned toward the person to apologize, whoever it was didn't pause. But I did as pins and needles pierced every inch of my skin. Instead of confronting a stranger, I saw a familiar figure half-hidden behind one of the booths. *Dayton?*

I stood frozen, people parting around me as I squinted to better glimpse the dark form. It was his shape but thinner. Panic laced my blood, just as it had so many times in our relationship. I took a hesitant step closer to be sure it was Dayton, but he was gone. Only the crowd that meandered along the pier remained. *Could I have imagined him?*

A few blinks to clear my eyes, and I looked again. I must have imagined him. The day had begun with stress and accusations. *Why wouldn't my mind instantly go to my ex?*

That made more sense. I pushed out a breath and turned to head back to the boat, doing my best to dismiss the way I'd felt when I'd thought it was him watching me.

A gentle breeze stirred my hair, and I enjoyed the sun's warmth. I loved the sound of the waves breaking along the shore as I walked adjacent to the beach. I was glad I'd decided to walk. It gave me time to think. Mr. Wilder was trouble, and without Kylian running defense, I wasn't up for round two. Not if it would mess with my head and dredge up phantom glimpses of Dayton.

I had to keep reassuring myself that there was no way he'd found me. I would have known. *Right?* The article about Kylian's connection to me didn't even matter. The picture of me in Kylian's passenger seat wasn't clear, since I'd held up my hand to block my face. Only my hair was visible. I dismissed that. Dayton wouldn't have known it was me from that one incident. Besides, Science Barbie had been all over Kylian at the fundraiser. I was safe.

It helped, especially after he'd left me alone—with good reason. If he hadn't, I liked to think that I would have told him to go and maybe even to forget about the contract, that his mom's health and safety were so much more important. I didn't want to add to their stress. Maybe I should think about moving on, since my presence only infuriated his dad. And people like him were dangerous.

When I arrived at the dock, I leaned against one of the pillars and stared at Kylian's luxury sailboat, which I wouldn't be sleeping on anymore. It was for the best.

A shadow fell across me, and I jumped.

"Hey." Kylian laid his hand on the small of my back. "Are you okay?"

"Yeah, you just startled me." I cleared my throat, needing to say what had to be said. "I was going to get my stuff and head out." A strand of my hair danced in the wind, and I tucked it behind my ear.

"What are you talking about? I had to check on Mom, but she wasn't home. So I wanted to make sure my dad hadn't come back. He's not here."

"But for how long?" That man had an agenda. I knew people like him. There would be no stopping Danbury Wilder from getting what he wanted. It wasn't over. I should run, get away as quickly as I could. Definitely before the press got ahold of whatever story he would put out about me or find from snooping into my past.

"I don't know how long. It's probably not a good idea for us to stay on the boat tonight. I need to return to my mom's, and I want you to come with me."

"Are you sure? It might be easier for you if I left and you made the same deal with that girl your dad wants you involved with." I refused to name Science-Nerd Barbie.

"No. That's not happening. We made a deal, and I'm holding you to it. My dad will move on. He made his point, and I made mine."

I got the sense that there was more to the story, but I left it alone, deciding to trust him instead. Sinking into his side, I borrowed his strength. I felt safe with him and didn't want to ruin it by pressuring him about details or what came next. "Okay, just let me grab my stuff."

With my bag stowed in his SUV, he drove us to his mom's

place. Leaning back against my seat, I studied him. Tension rolled off him in waves.

"Can you get notes for your missed classes?"

"Yeah, I got it covered. This is more important. I can't skip practice, though."

"I can stay with her when you have to leave." I shrugged. "It'll be good to hang out with her anyway, and I can cook."

"That would work." He grinned then pulled into an open spot about a block from his mom's brownstone.

We didn't say anything more as we hurried from the SUV and into her building. While we waited for her door to open, I struggled to not let him hear how out of breath I was after climbing all those stairs—at his superhuman speed—without using the railing to pull myself up. I mentally rolled my eyes because, of course, Mr. Superstar Athlete wasn't suffering with me.

The door opened, and Kylian's mom's joyful smile settled my discomfort.

"Well, isn't this a nice surprise? I didn't expect you today." She stepped aside. "Come in."

A tremor ran through Kylian's body as he hugged his mom. I rubbed my chest, trying to ease the ache at seeing someone who exuded so much confidence look scared, despite the way he shouldered his dad's threats with ease.

I shut the door behind us and stepped fully inside the apartment. Kylian ushered his mom to the couch and sat beside her, angling so they faced each other. I leaned against the door, not knowing what to do.

"Dad hasn't stopped by or called, has he?" Kylian stretched his arm along the back of the couch.

"No." Evalyn pulled her discarded blanket over her legs, her eyes narrowing. "Why?"

"He's threatening to kick you out."

"What do you mean?" Her voice sharpened, and I shifted

from foot to foot. "Explain. Don't hide anything from me. It'll only come back around to blindside us if you do. And, Gia, please have a seat, hon."

I took the only other seat in the room, her recliner, which she probably spent the most time in. It felt wrong to sit there, to be a part of the intimate moment between mother and son. *But if I were his fiancée for real, wouldn't I be present for something like this?* I held as still as possible, trying not to be a distraction.

Kylian didn't waste time. He relayed what had happened at the campaign fundraiser his father had asked him to attend and his pressure on Kylian to make one of his benefactors happy by threatening to throw Evalyn out on the street. "I can't imagine he'll do it. Displacing you would make him look bad."

Evalyn scoffed. "You're right. No man who wants to be a senator will risk bad press by tossing his terminally ill ex-wife to the curb." She laid a hand against his cheek. "I'm proud of you, but maybe we should talk about this wedding, since everyone in the room knows it's not real."

"Mom."

My mouth fell open, and I met his apologetic gaze with my wide one.

"No offense to you, dear." Evalyn took in my shocked expression and grimaced. "You're lovely, and I would love nothing more than to call you my daughter-in-law, but the timing is suspect, and I know my son. He'll do anything to make me happy."

"Our engagement is real, Mom." Kylian's voice didn't even waver. "Maybe we would have waited to set the date until after I settled in whatever city and team I sign with, but there are extenuating circumstances."

I sucked in a slow breath, appreciating how he didn't say what those were—not only about his mom's terminal illness but my homeless situation.

"We can talk about it later." She leaned against the couch as if it took too much strength to sit up without its aid.

"Evalyn." I cleared my throat to get rid of how shaky my voice sounded. "I would love nothing more than to be a part of your family."

"In my heart, you already are, Gia." She smiled, stood slowly, then bent to hug me. "I'm tired, but you're both welcome to stay. I'm going to take a nap." She turned to Kylian at the entrance to the hallway that led to what were probably the bedrooms. "Don't worry about your father. He won't throw me out and risk the press catching wind of his actions. He's not that stupid."

We didn't say anything until her door clicked softly closed, telling us she was out of earshot.

"I'll stay here while you go to practice. If he shows up, I'll threaten to go to the press."

Kylian stood and crossed the distance between us in two long strides. I was in his arms before I knew his intentions. I sank into his embrace, shaken from the day's events. I was still stunned by what a raging asshole his father was. *But... politics.* I should have assumed he was a jerk behind the façade.

"Thank you."

The deep rumble of his voice traveled through his chest and into mine. I couldn't control the shiver that raced up my spine, telegraphing too loudly for my peace of mind the effect his touch had on me.

"We'll stay here tonight." He released me and moved toward the door, pausing with his hand on the knob. "I'll try to get back as soon as I can."

I shrugged. "You don't need to rush. I'll make dinner for your mom and hang out with her this evening." Honestly, I was glad we were staying there. I was entirely too freaked out about the guy I'd seen on the dock. He'd looked at me oddly. I could have imagined it, but the way my skin crawled, I didn't think so.

"Don't worry about anything, okay?"

I nodded, questions poised on the tip of my tongue. He'd told his mom our relationship was real and that we planned to get married earlier because of the circumstances. I wanted to ask him when because I was almost desperate for the protection he offered. I rubbed my hand over my heart for the second time as he left with instructions for me to lock the door behind him. Doing that simple task was easier than addressing the weird ache in my chest and what it meant.

CHAPTER TWENTY-THREE

KYLIAN

Practice was brutal but good. I needed it. We were ready for the game against Alabama, and I was determined to make that the defining moment to get a foothold in the NFL. The right scouts would be there. The buzz under my skin made it tight as I entered Mom's apartment. It was late. After practice, I had film to watch. Mom was used to it, and Gia never complained about how much time I put into football—*but why would she?*

I shook my head, struggling not to confuse the relationship more than I had. I craved her. I even liked her. But too much was at stake, and I couldn't get carried away. No matter how much I'd come to care about or desire her, Mom's well-being was the most important thing—and that was being threatened.

Dad had left a message while I was at practice, and after what had happened that morning, I returned the call.

"What do you want?" was my opening when he answered.

"Getting down to business, good." Dad chuckled. "We have that in common."

"Doubtful." I was nothing like him. Never would be.

"I'm offering, for the last time, to pay for your mom's treatments if you drop this girl and take up with Melanie Honeycutt. If you don't, I'll find any dirt in that girl's background and destroy her. And as for your mother... well, I don't think you need me to spell that one out."

Fuck. I hated him with everything in me. No one mattered to him. Everything he did was for his own gain. This conversation got to me more than the others had, and I felt myself giving in, too worried about paying for Mom's treatments. I didn't want to give up on Gia, but I couldn't figure any other way out of his demands. "Fine. I'll date Melanie—after you make a lump-sum payment to keep Mom in the treatment program for the next six months."

"Deal. I'll have my assistant send over the payment confirmation once it's done. But only after I see you out with Melanie and get a report from her father."

He had me by the balls—*this time.* I couldn't do, or say, anything else, so I hung up. The weight of what I had to do was almost too much to bear—or it was until I thought about what would happen to Mom and Gia if I didn't go along with his demands.

Things were out of control, and my gut clenched from the terms we'd discussed. At some point, I would have to tell Gia about the tentative deal I'd made. It didn't change the one I had with her, except it did. She would still get the money, and Mom's treatment would be paid for, keeping her in the experimental program. Not only that—Dad had threatened Gia and backed me into a corner. I couldn't let her suffer because of my fucking father.

I followed the soft glow of the kitchen light, stomach rumbling and curious to see who was awake. When I entered the tiny room, I stopped, surprised to see Mom at the table, wrapped in a blanket, with a glass of water in front of her.

"Couldn't sleep?" I forced myself to move as if nothing was bothering me. After gripping the door to the fridge, I opened it.

"No. Not after that bomb you dropped on me earlier." She stood and hip checked me like she used to. "Gia made a fabulous dinner. Even with my limited appetite, I had to eat some of it."

"Really? That good, huh?"

She gave me a sly look. "You should know."

I should, but I didn't. And Mom couldn't know that. "She's practically a chef. I'm not surprised her food made you hungry."

I moved back so Mom could pull out the plate they must've made for me. She set it in the microwave, hit a few buttons, and returned to her seat. I busied myself getting some water then the food from the microwave before sitting at the table with her. The loud growl from my stomach made Mom chuckle. I dug in. She was right. Gia knew what she was doing.

"Why don't you tell me what's going on?"

My fork halted halfway to its destination. I wrestled with wanting to shove it in my mouth or answering the impossible question. The steely look in her eyes had me putting the fork down and giving her my full attention.

"You can't keep shielding me, Kylian. I've been dealing with your father a lot longer than you have."

"Why is that? With how selfish and manipulative he is, why did you choose him?" The words were out before I could stop them. "I'm sorry."

She waved away my apology and tucked a few strands of hair behind her ear before letting her hand fall back onto her lap.

"It's just... you're opposites. And from what I can tell, you don't have any common interests."

"We have you."

I snorted, and a rueful smile curved her lips.

"Your dad is very handsome, and I knew he was going places when I married him. I thought we had the same goals and similar enough dreams. Other than having you and your pursuits, I came to realize that we didn't." She pursed her lips.

"When the going got tough, he left, which was fine. I'm glad I didn't have to share you. Every moment was a blessing."

I hated it when she said things like that last part. It always felt like she was saying goodbye, and the idea of living without her was more than I could take.

"Now, I've answered your question. Why don't you tell me what else is bothering you because it's written all over you?"

I scrubbed my hands over my face, wishing she couldn't read me so well. But if anyone could make sense of the corner Dad had backed me into, it was her. "He's forced me to make a deal that will hurt Gia. I don't want to do it, but the apartment that you're living in depends on it. And… he's going to dig into her past with the intent to destroy her. I don't have a choice." I didn't want to go into the money problem and her treatments.

"You don't have a choice about what?" Her sharp voice cut into the thick of the problem. "This is just a place."

"But it means so much to you. Whenever I try to get you to move, you tell me it's where you want to be and nothing will change that."

"I do like it here. There are just so many memories and good neighbors. They're friends. We look out for one another. I never wanted to invade your college world, not like that."

"Mom." I leaned forward and gave her hand a brief squeeze. "You wouldn't."

She drew in a long, slow breath before releasing it. "Let's circle back to the heart of the problem. You always have a choice, especially where your father is concerned. Don't let him threaten what you might have with Gia."

Might. She still wasn't convinced Gia and I were in a relationship. And she was right. It was fake, but it sure as hell felt real.

"Whatever deal you made with him, forget it. You let me worry about that man. I have an arsenal of secrets I'm not afraid to use if he tries to hurt you. Nobody, Illinois senatorial candidate or not, will hurt my kid." She stood and kissed me on the cheek. "I'm heading to bed. I suggest you do the same." Pausing in the doorway, she narrowed her eyes, and the fire returned that had been there before all the rounds of chemo. "Let me handle him, and you'll see that everything will be fine."

I stretched out my legs and rolled my shoulders, easing the tension. As I shoveled down the rest of my dinner, I wished I could believe everything would be okay, but I didn't. I knew my dad, and when he wanted something as badly as he did this, nothing would stand in his way—not even family.

After washing my dishes and putting them away, I shut off the light and carefully went through the living room and down the short hallway until I was at my door. No light shone underneath. Slowly, I opened it and slipped inside. The blinds were up, and moonlight slanted through the window, spilling over Gia's sleeping form. She lay curled on her side, her face turned toward me. I gently set down my bag, but the scuffing sound must've woken her because her eyelids fluttered open.

She sat up, drawing her knees to her chest and wrapping her arms around them. "You can turn on the light."

I hesitated momentarily, preferring to keep my secrets in the dark, but they would inevitably come out. She deserved to know. I flipped the switch, and she blinked a few times, adjusting to the change.

"Your dad never stopped by," she said while I moved closer, sitting on the edge of the bed.

"How was your time with Mom?" I was stalling but also genuinely wanted to know.

"Great." A soft smile curved her lips. "I cooked for her and told her stories about living with my uncle, and she shared some hilarious ones about you."

"I bet she did."

Her smile fell away at my flat tone. "What happened?"

Better to rip off the Band-Aid. "My dad forced me into the

deal. I'm going to date Melanie, then he thinks I'll eventually propose. I need to find a way out of it, but for now, I have to go along with his crazy scheme. You don't need to worry. I'll still pay the contract, and you can live on the boat for as long as you need," I rushed ahead to assure her when her face shuddered. I hated it. I wanted to feel her warmth, not the wall she erected between us again.

I hated hurting her, but I needed to protect her from my dad, and he was gunning for her—and Mom—if I didn't fall in line.

"Here."

She slid the ring halfway off her finger, but I stopped her, my hand covering hers. It bothered me, a lot. *Why?* All I knew was that I wanted the ring to stay where it was. "No. Don't. I'll find a way out of this. I just can't see it yet." I pushed the ring back up her finger, wishing my immediate situation was different. I was juggling too many things. At least with her wearing my ring, I had hope I would find a way out of my dad's tangled web.

Her lower lip trembled, stealing the air from my lungs. Then she pinched her lips together. I curled my fingers around her arm, but she moved, and my hand fell to the bed.

The feelings were so foreign but impossible to ignore. Things had gone too far between us. Somehow, she'd gotten past my walls. With a jolt of panic, I realized I'd fallen for her.

CHAPTER TWENTY-FOUR

GIA

It shouldn't bother me. My fingers curled, nails biting into the skin of my palms. It did. *Kylian is going to date someone else.*

I'd sat up and moved so my back rested against the headboard. He'd turned the light on, and now I wished he hadn't. The moonlight would have been enough. I didn't want him to scrutinize my every reaction for this conversation.

"I don't think it'll come to me having to marry her."

I snorted a laugh. "You believe that? It won't be a neat little contract like we have." I had to take a beat. Calm down until my features were schooled to hide the absolute turmoil in my mind and body. *How did I let myself catch feelings for him?* "I saw her reaction to you in the school's blog video. That woman will not let you go without a fight, and I suspect she has the means for a ruthless battle."

His firm lips pinched tightly together, and a muscle jumped along his sharp jawline. "I don't want anything to do with her. The problem is my dad. Mom is in an experimental treatment program that insurance doesn't cover. I don't have enough money to keep paying for the appointments. My dad will only continue to help if I do what he wants."

"Oh." The argument left me. His father was terrible, and I could understand why Kylian felt backed into a corner. "I'll, um, I'll go to the boat in the morning and get the rest of my stuff. You don't need to worry about me or the contract. We can just forget it." He had bigger things than the deal we'd made. I wanted to say that sleeping with him was a mistake, but I couldn't. It wasn't.

"No." He growled. "I want you to stay. I can uphold that end of our agreement."

Anger whipped through me. "I'm not staying there. Your dad or that woman will find out and kick me out anyway. I would much rather leave on my terms. And if I go early enough, I won't have to deal with any photographers hanging around in case your dad leaks anything about me." That was one thing solved.

"I won't let them." Steel infused his voice, and his eyes flashed with determination. "Trust me, there is no way they'll kick you out, especially if I do what my dad wants." He moved closer, but when I shook my head, he stopped. "If you left, I would worry about you. Please stay on the boat for as long as you need."

It was a touching offer, a good one even. But I couldn't let Mad-Scientist Barbie toss me out—I recognized the danger there. And I had too much pride to let that happen. I knew he would assume I'd agreed to stay, but I just said, "Thank you."

His features smoothed, some of the tension leaving his body. The muscle along his jaw stopped jumping. "I'll sleep on the couch."

"That would be best." I uncurled my hands and tucked them under the sheet to hide the tremor that ran through them.

In my head, I counted down from ten, trying to ignore how his presence saturated the room, making it seem smaller than it was. He filled the doorway as he let himself out. I waited, needing him to be farther from the room before I let the first tear fall.

It hurt that he was throwing away... *what?* I lay down and punched the pillow. We weren't anything other than a business agreement that had gone too far. I never should have slept with him. It had blurred the line we were trying to maintain, muddying it with feelings—probably only on my part. Maybe I should just look at it as though I'd dodged a bullet.

Stupid feelings. *And why does he want me to keep the ring if his sights are on Blondie?* I curled into a ball, hating how alone I felt. One night. I swiped the wetness from the corners of my eyes. I would feel sorry for myself for one night, then I had to do what needed to be done, since the only person I could rely on was myself. Something Kylian had made very clear in that conversation, despite how much I'd softened and let him into my traitorous heart.

I willed my eyes to shut, but it didn't do much good. I tossed and turned most of the night.

When morning rolled around, I dragged myself from the bed and tiptoed to the bathroom to get ready. I had everything packed, which wasn't much. Ignoring the dark circles under my eyes, I entered the family room and found Kylian waiting for me on the couch.

A dark-blue T-shirt stretched across his broad shoulders, highlighting the sculpted muscles of his chest and abdomen. When I met his gaze, I was mildly appeased by the circles under his eyes too.

"I left Mom a note." He stood, towering over me. "I'll drive you to the boat."

I nodded, not wanting to prolong staying there and risking her waking. I'd had fun hanging out with her the previous day, and I could easily see myself doing that often. But he'd tossed me aside for a better deal. I didn't blame him for protecting his mom, but it still stung.

Kylian opened the door and motioned for me to precede him. I waited for him to lock it behind us, then we walked the hallway to the stairs in silence, my thoughts whirling the entire way. Tense silence hung thickly between us as we navigated the stairs then outside his mom's apartment building.

The days had run together. I could barely keep track of where we were in the week. But I knew he had somewhere to be. It was a game day. A big one, from what he'd told me. "You have to be at the stadium soon?"

"Yeah." He glanced at his phone while holding the passenger door open for me. "I have some time before I need to leave."

I got into the SUV and tossed my purse and bag on the floor at my feet. As he went around the side and got in, I looked out the window, needing space between us in any way I could find. Traffic wasn't bad due to the early hour. The Ferris wheel loomed high in the skyline as we neared the harbor.

He parked in the lot reserved for boaters, and we got out and headed toward the dock where the *Quarterback Keeper* was tethered. The carnival was still set up but hadn't been opened to the public yet that day. People milled about, getting the booths ready. A shiver ran down my spine, unease lingering from who I'd thought I'd seen the previous day.

Enough people filled the space that we had to weave through them. I moved faster, dislodging his large hand from my back. I couldn't stand to have him touch me or be too close. The last thing I wanted was to break down. I was stronger than that. I had survived so much that his nearness shouldn't bother me— but it did. I was barely holding it together, which didn't make sense. He shouldn't mean that much to me. It was a business deal. I had to remember that.

I tucked some hair behind my ear and let him help me onto

the boat. A shiver traveled down my spine from how close he was behind me. I punched in the code and frowned when it appeared as if it was already unlocked. Maybe it was just me. I didn't trust my perception with how blindsided I felt by Kylian bowing to his father's demands—even if the reason was justifiable.

I hurried down the stairs then stood for a moment. That was it, the last time I would be on his boat. It had felt like a home, someplace I could rely on, and it had become that even more when he'd stayed with me.

Movement pulled my focus, and I turned toward Kylian, who sat on the edge of the banquette. "You don't have to stay. I know you need to get to the stadium."

"I don't feel right about leaving things this way, Gia."

I shivered, not just from his deep voice but because something felt off. My eye shifted to the counter. *Didn't I leave the chips out?* "Did you put the chips away?"

"Huh? No."

I scanned the galley. Everything was where it should be, but it seemed different—touched somehow. I wrapped my arms around my waist, an unwanted memory rising to the surface from the first time Dayton had cracked me across the face. He'd left the milk out, and I'd bitched at him about it. It was my first mistake. He was so furious that I'd spoken to him that way. According to him, it was my job to keep things tidy. I cradled the side of my face as if still feeling how hard he'd hit me. My lip had bled, and a bruise had formed soon after.

Cleaning up after him had been my job, and I'd had to be damn perfect about it. I absently rubbed the phantom pain in my wrist—the same one Dayton had broken for me not going to the client lunch with him like he wanted.

"Who the fuck are you?"

Kylian's snarl had me whirling to face him, my heart in my throat. His fierce gaze was caught on something over my shoulder. That hated minty smell wafted over me. My body locked down hard, fear crawling like angry fire ants over my skin. I felt *him* behind me, close enough that his breath disturbed my hair. My eyes closed, and my mouth opened slightly on an uneven exhalation.

How did Dayton find me?

"You should ask who Aurora is. I'm dying to hear the story she tells people."

Pain exploded across the back of my scalp from the brutal grip on my hair. Dayton shoved me, and I fell into the seat opposite Kylian. The pain meant nothing. There would be more. I scrambled to see Dayton. I knew it was better to keep him in my sights. But when I did, my blood ran cold. He had a gun pointed at us.

CHAPTER TWENTY-FIVE

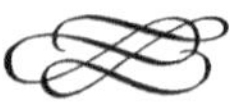

KYLIAN

"Dayton, please." Gia held out her palm, pleading. "You don't have to do this."

I remained seated—for the time being—and kept my gaze trained on Dayton, calculating everything about his posture, looking for an opening to rush him. He was big and muscular but probably not an athlete—more of a tool who kept himself in shape. From the corner of my eye, Gia—no, Aurora—trembled visibly. I would process who she really was and her connection to the abuser later. One thing was for sure—I wouldn't let the fucker hurt her.

"I don't care who you are. You need to get the fuck off my boat before I call the cops." It was a ballsy thing to say with a gun pointed at us. At least it would get his focus off her and onto me.

My jaw clenched harder at Dayton's laugh, and he swung the gun in my direction. I just needed an opening to attack. I'd been tackled by bigger and better than him on the field. He didn't compare to the giant linemen I faced down every Saturday. The only issue was his weapon.

"Come on, Dayton. Stop this. Let him go. He doesn't matter."

Gia scooted forward, one hand gripping the table, and she shook so hard, I felt the vibration in my arm where it rested on the solid surface. "He means nothing to me—I swear—just a meal ticket. I'll go with you. I promise."

I sprang into action when Dayton's focus shifted, launching myself into him. Shoulder planted into his midsection, I drove him back. My hand curled around his wrist. As he stumbled from the force behind my tackle, I rammed his hand onto the edge of the sink. Once, twice, then the gun clattered to the floor.

"Get out, Gia!" I yelled over Dayton's roar as we wrestled for control.

He slammed a cabinet door into my face then pulled open a drawer between us. Even with my attention divided between him and her, nothing would stop me from winning that fight.

He buried his fist in my stomach, and the corner of the counter bit into my hip. My attempt to get Gia out had been enough of a distraction for Dayton to take advantage. We traded punches. The guy was strong but didn't have finesse. He missed more than he connected. The satisfying crunch beneath my fist resonated through me as his nose cracked.

Cabinet doors hung askew, drawer contents littering the floor. Dayton used what he could as a distraction. I pinned him against the counter, twisted, then locked my arm around his neck. He fumbled through the drawers, rooting for whatever weapon he could find while I shouted at Gia. She wasn't moving fast enough.

"Go!"

She stumbled past us, and my attention wavered as pain pierced my side. My grip loosened at the flash of metal as he pulled a knife from me. He fucking stabbed me. My hand closed around his wrist, and I squeezed. The knife fell. In the back of my mind, I wondered what the hell Gia had been through at the hands of that monster.

I didn't move for a beat, and he took advantage of the puncture wound. I should have planted my feet better. I hadn't, and he got the upper hand, twisting my right arm hard behind me then slamming an elbow down on my shoulder. Blinding pain shot through my joint, traveling down my extremities and locking me in place. Blood poured from the wound at my side. I couldn't process the damage he'd done with that second attack. Not yet. I had too much at stake.

He released my arm, and I stumbled back when he lunged for her. I kicked his ankle, and he went down. So did she. Her head cracked against the doorjamb. It happened so fast. I moved to help her, but Dayton got in my face, the gun in his hand once more. I jolted in front of Gia to block her, keeping a visual of him from the corner of my eye. He swung. I felt the blow to the back of my head, then everything went dark.

CHAPTER TWENTY-SIX

~~Gia~~

Aurora

I struggled to open my eyes. My wrists were trapped in a viselike hold. I blinked, willing my mind to work. My arms were stretched over my head, and my body scraped along the floor as someone dragged me.

Everything that had happened before I'd hit my head flooded back. Dayton had found me. The gun. The fight between him and Kylian. My body jostled over stairs, and I went into immediate action, twisting, pulling, and shouting to get free.

Then I saw Kylian—slumped over, unconscious, and bleeding from a knife wound. He was losing a lot of blood. He needed help. Blind panic shot through me, and I resumed my efforts to break free, giving it everything I had.

I leaned my head back as Dayton managed to pull me up the stairs, his hands tight around my wrists. So much stronger than I was, he yanked me to my feet. This was bad. Wrenching my arms behind my back, he crushed me against his chest. I opened my mouth to scream.

"Shut the fuck up, Aurora. You brought this on yourself."

"Let me go, and I won't tell anyone what you did or who you are." I trembled as he laughed. "This won't end well for you. You know that, right?"

He leaned down, his nose against my neck. As he dragged it along the curve, inhaling, I shuddered. He made me physically sick.

"You smell like him."

His anger before was nothing compared to what I heard in his voice. My instincts flared, and I scanned the area, looking for help. I found none. No boaters topside or people close enough to see what was happening. He was going to kill me. I had to escape.

He shuffled me awkwardly forward along the deck. A pronounced limp slowed our progress, and strain etched groves that bracketed Dayton's scowl. Kylian had done some damage. I enjoyed the cruel smile that curved my lips. Dayton tightened his grip as he struggled to control me and get us off the boat.

Sun glinted off the rippling water as we neared the edge, sparking an idea. Dayton hated the water. We never went to the beach back in California, or even the pool, and I'd learned the reason why—he couldn't swim.

I knew what I had to do, but I was nervous. The circumstances called for drastic measures, though, and I pushed aside my anxiety, focusing on freeing an arm from his too-tight grip. I hoped I could shove him and run for help.

He changed his hold and pulled me against him. The steel band of his arm bit into my waist and held me flush against him as he jumped off the boat and onto the dock with a pained grunt. He'd taken most of the impact when our feet had hit the pier. I couldn't let that go to waste. It was my chance.

My gaze met a blissful stretch of water, and hope surged. A

gap stood where another boat should've been tied opposite Kylian's on the pier. Rope conveniently hung from one of the pilings, and I stretched my arms until my fingers gained purchase. Dayton found his balance and attempted to secure me against his body again, but I twisted and popped my hip into his. His arms loosened slightly as he released another grunt. In the small space, I turned until we were mostly facing one another then kicked his injured knee, using my body's momentum to fully yank out of his grasp.

I had one chance to do it right and get rid of him. With all the strength I could muster, I rammed my shoulder into him. He released me, arms flailing as he stumbled to the dock's edge. His heel missed the pier, meeting air instead. Grossly off balance with only his injured leg on the dock, he lost the battle and tumbled into Lake Michigan.

The sound of his body hitting the water sent a bolt of satisfaction through me. *Stay there.* If he couldn't get to the pier's pilings, I had a shot of being rid of him for good.

As he gasped and flailed, panic and guilt constricted my lungs. I didn't want to feel bad, but I did. His head went under. He broke the surface, coughing and sputtering twice, three times, then nothing. The water's surface returned to the gentle lap of waves as if nothing violent had happened moments ago. I sucked in a stuttering breath, and tears flooded my eyes at what I'd done. I would face consequences, but I couldn't think about it with Kylian lying in a pool of blood below deck.

The pounding in my head from hitting it was nothing compared to the sound of my feet as I whirled around, jumped back onto the boat deck, and sprinted across it. Kylian needed medical attention. A sob broke from my trembling lips. I was terrified to see how much blood he'd lost.

I flew down the short flight of stairs to where he lay on the floor. Blood from his side wound soaked his gray T-shirt.

"Where's your phone?"

"Pocket," he croaked then winced as he tried to move his right arm to help.

Worry made time slip. It slowed then raced forward. I was so scared, and I didn't like the lack of color in his skin. His eyes closed, and terror shot through me.

"Stay with me, QB1." My breaths sawed in and out as I tried to keep him conscious and dial 911. I tapped his cheek with my palm when his eyes didn't open. "Hey, open your eyes."

He grunted then slurred, "Stop it."

Tears ran unchecked down my cheeks. "Please don't die on me." I grabbed some towels from one of the drawers and carefully applied as much pressure as I thought was okay. I couldn't tell if any vital organs had been punctured. I only hoped it didn't cost Kylian his life. And on the heels of that thought, I glanced at his arm—*could that injury cause the potential loss of his football career?*

The operator's voice was like a lifeline. I told her about Kylian's knife wound and that he'd lost a lot of blood. Between sobs, I somehow managed to convey that we were on the *Quarterback Keeper*.

"I never should have come into your life. I'm so sorry."

"Who is he?" Kylian's words were thin, weak, and still managed to convey a wealth of fury.

I sucked in a shaky breath and pulled myself together as much as possible. He deserved to know the truth. So I told him everything but in a truncated version of the story. "I made a mistake. Dayton is my abusive ex."

"Husband?"

"No. Thankfully. And he shouldn't bother you ever again."

Kylian's eyes caught mine, and I shivered at their heat. I knew Kylian would have come out on top if Dayton hadn't stabbed him.

"I, ah, I pushed him off the pier. He can't swim."

Silence. Kylian said nothing.

Does he think I'm a murderer? I shifted my weight on my knees. Whatever, I would do it again if I had the chance. Uncomfortable with Kylian's unwavering stare, I rambled. "He was bad news, the wrong guy at the right time. I came to Chicago trying to lose him. It didn't work. I'll tell you more about it when you're well." I kept my voice as soft and soothing as possible, trying to keep us calm. "I was still in college, and he was this wealthy, good-looking guy who was into me. Anyway, we dated for a few months. After a while, I moved in with him. That's when the signs became glaringly obvious that I was in way over my head. He was possessive, jealous, and controlling. When I tried to break up with him and move out, he showed me exactly what would happen if I attempted to leave him. But I left anyway. When I did, I hid who I was and moved as far from him as possible. I don't know how he found me. The pictures on the blog weren't that clear, and I didn't use my real name. I'm just… God, Kylian. I'm so sorry this happened to you and that you got dragged into my chaos."

A thump sounded overhead then footsteps. "Hello? Paramedics."

"Down here. Hurry, please!"

Two men in dark clothes thundered down the steps. At the sight of help approaching, my shaking that had never entirely left kicked up a notch. They crowded around Kylian, and I moved out of the way as they worked on him. One of them turned to assess me.

I brushed him off. "I'm fine. I don't need anything."

He looked like he might argue, but I shifted away and pointed at Kylian. With indecision warring in his eyes, he finally turned back to help his partner. The police arrived, and I braced myself for the questions that were sure to come.

The older gentleman with gray peppering his dark temples glanced my way. "We're going to move him now. You'll have to follow us to the hospital."

CHAPTER TWENTY-SEVEN

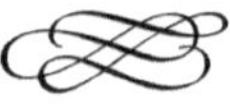

AURORA

*K*ylian *is undergoing emergency surgery because of me.* Tears streamed down my face as I rushed through the hospital, following the directions from the information desk to the waiting room. My hands shook as I shoved his keys into my pocket. I couldn't process what was happening.

It'd taken more time than I would have liked to leave the harbor, due to questions from the police taking my statement. I'd made them wait for answers until I'd called Kylian's mom. I didn't even remember the hospital drive, but I'd finally made it.

After a few turns, I closed in on the waiting room, desperate to talk to a doctor or nurse to learn if Kylian was out yet and how he was doing. A shadow fell across me, and I jerked to the left in the hallway to avoid colliding with a man. Instead of moving, he blocked me. I lifted my gaze then sucked in a stuttering breath at the man who barred my path—Danbury Wilder. Kylian's father towered over me, a calculating gleam in his eyes.

"How—"

"My ex-wife called about our son. I happened to be close by." He cupped my elbow and backed me up then dragged me around a corner leading down another hallway farther from my destination. "Before you go anywhere near my son, we have a few things to discuss, young lady."

I yanked my arm out of his grasp. "Young lady" was a far cry from what he'd called me before, but it didn't matter, since he made it sound just as vile. "We have nothing to talk about... unless you've heard how Kylian is doing."

"He's in surgery. That's all you need to know."

"Look"—I took a step back—"I'm—"

"Spare me the ridiculous sob story about how you care for Kylian," Mr. Wilder growled, advancing a step closer. "I want you gone from my son's life."

I shook my head. I wouldn't let him bully me into running off.

"If you fail to do as I say, the repercussions will fall squarely on your head."

"What are you talking about?" I was sick to my stomach. I couldn't understand how such a horrible man had any relation to someone as incredible as Kylian.

Mr. Wilder's lips peeled back, and he bared his teeth, his anger palpable. "Here's what's going to happen. You'll leave right now. Evalyn and I will be the only ones to see Kylian after his surgery. You'll visit him in a few days to tell him you are no longer interested in a relationship. I don't care how you do it, but you will extricate yourself from his life. And there can't be any doubt in his mind that you are ending things. Make it convincing."

My head jerked back as if he'd slapped me. "No. I won't do that." I clasped my hands before me, trembling more than I wanted the monster to witness. *What could he possibly do?*

"I see you need more convincing." Mr. Wilder's cold eyes hardened. "If you fail to do as I say, I'll make sure Evalyn is booted from the treatment program where she's finally seeing positive results. The cancer will ravage her body again, and her imminent death will be on your conscience."

He wouldn't. I wanted to call his bluff because that had to be what was going on. "You've already paid for the next few treatments, and Kylian's going into the NFL. He'll take over then."

"Is that what you think?" His brows climbed his forehead. "You're partially right. My son is an elite athlete and will make it into the NFL, but only if he gets the proper treatment for the injuries you're responsible for. Make no mistake about it, young lady. You brought this on yourself when you invited your violent and unstable former boyfriend into his life."

"I didn't—"

"You did." He scoffed. "None of that would have happened to Kylian if not for you."

Tears flooded my eyes again, and I widened them in a desperate attempt to keep the tears from falling. *He's right.* Still, I didn't want to let him see how much his words slammed into me with the force of a battering ram. "Kylian doesn't see it the same way." I hoped he didn't. *He knew I would never intentionally put him in harm's way, didn't he?*

"I can see the wheels turning. You need to stop. Do whatever it takes to break things off with my son when you see him in a couple of days. If you don't, you will be responsible for Evalyn's demise and my son losing his dream of going into the NFL— and you know that's been his lifelong ambition."

I had some fight left in me, very little, but what I did possess, I flung his way. "You have no bearing on keeping him from the NFL."

"Did you know he suffered a torn rotator cuff in his throwing arm?" He saw from my shock that I didn't. "He'll need intensive physical therapy, and as an athlete, he'll want to do anything and everything in his power to heal and get back on that field. That means platelet-rich plasma injections, which are very pricey and not covered by insurance. If you're gone from his life, I'll pay for everything. My son will only have the best care money can buy, which will save his career. If not..."

Bile climbed my throat, and I backed away from him. I couldn't do anything. Not a goddamned thing. Hurting Evalyn and Kylian because I wanted to be in their lives was not worth the hell Kylian's father would unleash if I stayed. I was almost at the exit before he stopped me.

"Do we have a deal?"

God help me, but yes, we did. I could only nod before I turned and fled.

CHAPTER TWENTY-EIGHT

KYLIAN

Several days passed while I was stuck in the hospital. Everything I'd worked for was gone. Dark despair hung like a heavy mantle on my shoulders. Football had been my world, my end game, how I'd coped with things. And it was gone. Or that was what the doc said. *Fuck that—I'll prove him wrong.*

My mind wrestled with the potential loss of my future, the inability to protect my mom from my father, and the reality of Gia's situation. *Where is she?*

I felt as if I were underwater, drowning. My mind tried to swim through the murky, heavy depth of each failure that had brought me to my current state—the inability to protect Gia and Mom. Then there was that other thing.

I always knew Gia was holding something back, and I should have pressed her to find out what. I'd wanted to help her. I understood why she'd withheld her past from me, even if I didn't like it. But if I'd known what she'd faced, maybe I wouldn't have ended up in a fucking hospital bed, after surgery, missing out on the Alabama game and who the hell knew how many more.

I'd needed that game. My mom needed it. *Now that I'm red-shirted, how the hell will I get the money for her treatments and get out from under my dad's thumb?*

Injuries like mine had the potential to end careers. The doc's prediction wouldn't leave my head. He'd said that the tear to my right rotator cuff could cause a considerable problem with mobility if it didn't heal correctly, and he was worried it might not. Then there was the puncture wound to my kidney, which they'd had to do emergency surgery on to save my life. The shoulder injury shouldn't cost me football, but it could. He was wrong—I would play again, better than before. I couldn't let the setback stop me from helping my mom when she needed me the most.

ESPN had reported my injury and surgery, sharing it far and wide to all coaches' and scouts' ears. I was achingly aware of the potential reduction in the contract value I would receive when I came back—and I would—if I even got picked up by a team.

And Gia—*no, Aurora*—had suffered at that asshole's hands too. Bile climbed my throat at the thought of him abusing her. Relief and pride had filled me at the sight of her falling to her knees to help me while I sat there in a pool of blood.

But what she'd said about me meaning nothing to her had gotten into my head. Even if it had been an attempt to save me. I'd trusted her with everything I cared about most, but she didn't trust me enough to give me her real name. *And she's not here. Did she ever care about me, or was I just a means to an end?*

The weight of my mom's fate was my priority, especially when my future lay in shambles around me. Because it wasn't only mine—it was my mom's ticket to health and freedom too.

I had a long road ahead of me with physical therapy and doing everything my docs said. Four to six months was the timeline. The doc said six. I would prove him wrong and do it in four.

I knew my head wasn't on straight, and maybe I wasn't

thinking clearly. But I knew how to achieve exactly one thing, and that was getting back in the game. I had to become a machine, solely focused on recovery.

Once I was back on the field, I would have to prove myself with a consistency I hadn't needed to worry about as much before. There would be no signing before the combine, not after my injury. I would have to get an invite to the combine and prove to the NFL teams that I had what it took to be a first-round draft pick.

"Stop it," Mom said, jolting me out of my dark thoughts.

"You shouldn't be here." I'd growled the words at her, and an instant wave of guilt hit me. She didn't deserve my bitterness. I had no right to take my emotions out on her. Or Aurora.

"Why? Because I spend too much time in the hospital already? I'm here, Kylian, and I'm not going away. So stop feeling sorry for yourself, and be the man I raised you to be."

Fuck. She raised me. I got the message loud and clear, and I turned my head and flashed her what I hoped was a convincing smile. Dad was in the waiting room, pandering to the press he'd allowed to accompany him. The hospital wouldn't let them near my room, but they didn't stop the circus going on not far from it. Nor did they stop the giant flower arrangement, courtesy of Melanie, then Dad's text scolding me for not letting her—my future wife, according to him—in to see me.

Dad was using me again. My misfortune generated headlines, and with my connection to Danbury Wilder, he was getting even more coverage, which only helped his campaign. The dull pain in my shoulder went ignored. I blocked as much of the bullshit from my dad as I could because Mom was right— she'd raised me. Not him. And she taught me not to wallow, or at least not for long. I had to pick myself back up and get to work. I had drive in spades, and nothing would stop me from achieving my goals.

"Ah, there he is." Mom's voice had softened as she stared at me, and the smile curving her mouth made her look younger than the disease ravaging her body usually allowed. Some color had returned to her face, even if her shoulder-length brown hair still looked dull. "He worked a miracle on your kidney and expects a full recovery. Focus on that. The damage to your shoulder wasn't as bad as it appeared. Don't listen to the general surgeon's worst-case scenario. You know the orthopedic doctor's prognosis is favorable. I know you. You'll overcome this. You'll miss games this year, but you still have your senior year and the combine then."

"It's not good enough. I need to be out there sooner. I'll use some of the money left from Grandad's trust for PRP injections."

Aurora had released me from the contract's terms the night before the fight with her ex. It felt wrong in the back of my mind, but I needed the money. I could help her in other ways. She would have a place to stay and my dad off her back, and I would make sure the fridge was stocked. And somehow, I would figure a way out of the Melanie deal so no obstacles would stop me from being with Aurora.

"Platelet-rich plasma injections might not get you there faster. But"—Mom sighed—"I support your decision. However, you're not going to use your trust fund. I'll talk to your father. He'll pay for that and stop pressuring you to do whatever stupid scheme he's concocted."

She must have seen the doubt written all over my face because when she squeezed my hand, that steely determination that colored so much of my childhood blazed from her eyes. If Mom wanted something to happen, she always made sure it did. I just hoped whatever plan she was cooking in that brain of hers wouldn't cause her body additional stress and a relapse.

"When do you speak to your docs?" Mom asked.

She'd had great news when I'd woken from surgery. And it was something that made me even more determined to fight for her and my dreams. Her terminal cancer was responding to the new treatment and shrinking. Her body was going into remission. She still had more treatments to undergo. We had bills to pay and living expenses to worry about. But for the first time, I had a hope that she might survive.

"Later this week," I said. "But don't worry about any of that. We got a win. We're going to focus on that and your recovery."

Mom's phone rang, and she squeezed my hand, whispering that it was her doctor's office and she would be back in a minute.

I clicked through a few channels on the TV until finally settling on a game show, and then a soft knock sounded. Everything in me relaxed when I spotted Aurora through the small window in the door.

"Hey." Relief at seeing her batted some of the darkness away, letting a sliver of sunlight warm my foggy brain. "Are you okay? I thought you were right behind the ambulance." *Three days ago.* It was ten in the morning, and I couldn't figure out what had detained her, but I'd been worried something had happened.

"Yeah, I-I'm sorry." She offered a shaky smile that didn't reach her eyes. "I wanted to see you, but your family was here, and I didn't want to intrude. Not after everything that happened."

"What are you talking about? I wanted you to come." My hand closed around hers, needing the anchor because she was acting strange. That same vibe from the beginning, when she would run rather than talk to me, emanated from her.

"I need to tell you something." She sniffed and yanked her hand free to swipe at her eyes. "I was scared. Desperate. But the truth is, I used you, and I can't keep doing that. I never should have gotten involved with you. I should have left when you found me on your boat and never made that deal."

I was stunned into silence. My world was already uncertain, thanks to my injuries, and I could barely process her words.

She trembled as she slid my engagement ring from her finger and turned my hand over to press it into my palm. My fingers closed around it automatically, the diamond biting into my flesh.

"I'm sorry." She choked on the words, whirled around, then fled from the room.

Stunned, I lay there, staring after her, unable to do a thing about her leaving. *She never cared about me?* Her words repeated through my head until I finally put two and two together. I might never play football again. It made sense. Her saying she didn't care at this precise moment. She must have found out about the doc's prognosis. He would have told her, since she was my fiancée.

The door opened slightly. Mom called after Aurora, then the door shut without coming in. Muffled voices filtered through. Trapped in the hospital bed, I had to endure parts of her speech all over again.

Seconds passed of blissful silence, then Mom entered my room, and I turned away, not wanting to see the sympathy in her gaze.

"I'm sorry, Kylian."

I made the mistake of looking at her, and she winced.

Her hand curled around mine. "I'm sure it's a misunderstanding."

My gut churned. It wasn't a misunderstanding. My growing concern had been right—she'd used me. Aurora had never loved me or felt any of the things that I had for her. I was a fool. I was tired of the games. I'd been played, but Mom needed to know everything so she could let go of Aurora too.

"It's not a misunderstanding. I need to tell you something." I met her eyes, letting her witness the truth in mine, no matter how painful. I was done with the lies. "Our relationship was fake. I got her to go along with it because she needed a place to stay and my boat was an easy solution for that." I explained the contract, the business agreement we had. "I'm sorry. I just wanted to give you everything you wanted so you wouldn't have to worry about me." *When you leave.* I couldn't say that part. I didn't know if I ever could.

"Oh, Kylian." Mom sighed, sadness flooding her eyes. "I only wanted to know you would be happy after I left. That you had someone to take care of and love you. I didn't mean to put so much pressure on you, and for that, I'm so very sorry. But—"

Another knock sounded, and a spike of irritation shot through me at the interruption. I clenched my jaw before I lashed out at whoever the visitor was.

A man entered, his gaze skimming over me then latching onto Mom. Interest sparked in his eyes, and a crooked grin curved his lips. It was enough to distract me from how my world was crumbling around me.

"Detective Lancaster." Mom's voice held a smile that was impossible to ignore.

I whipped my head around and narrowed my eyes. *What the heck?* I looked from her to the detective and noted something between them that I wasn't sure how to feel about. Mom was gorgeous, even while knocked down by illness. I shouldn't be surprised that the detective had noticed, but witnessing her positive response to the attention was oddly uncomfortable.

"How can I help you, Detective?" I'd already talked with him and his partner after surgery. The entire story of finding Dayton on the boat, the gun, our fight, and Aurora saying she pushed him into the lake had been relayed. I couldn't imagine what else he required.

"I wanted to stop by and give you an update."

"How nice of you to do that," Mom said.

So strange. My gaze darted between the two again. Mom was blushing.

"Yes, thanks. Did you find him?"

"No, not entirely. We haven't recovered the body yet. But we did locate a torn piece of his clothing twisted around a boat's propeller that Aurora identified as the shirt he was wearing. And the DNA from the finger we found matches Dayton's. We hope to recover the rest of him soon, since no one around the accident site saw a man emerge from the water. If he did survive, we'll find him. Aurora Mason, who also uses the alias Gia Mason, gave a statement about Dayton, including his last name and address."

"Okay." I wanted him to hurry up. Besides, I'd already spilled about Aurora's name.

The doc would be making rounds soon, and I needed to get a plan in place about when physical therapy would begin and how soon they thought I could return to the field for practice. It was important if I wanted to beat the tentative date for best-case circumstances they'd given me—by a lot. That was what I had to focus on. Recovery. Returning to the field better than ever. And helping Mom. Not a girl who never cared for me. Who only pretended to in order to use me.

The ring bit into my palm. The harder I worked, the less I would think about Aurora.

"We have every reason to believe that Dayton Vanderbilt is dead. If he did manage to survive, from what Aurora has told us, we don't think you would be in any further danger from him."

"But?" I knew I wouldn't like his answer because I still felt compelled to protect Aurora—that hadn't died, even if she didn't have feelings for me.

"Aurora could be if we don't locate him or his body. But we're doing everything we can to find him."

"And put him behind bars?" Mom snapped, echoing my thoughts.

Gone were the flirty looks. She'd returned to that ferocious mama-bear persona I'd experienced my whole life. It was only her sickness that had quelled it, which was why I'd worked so hard to protect her from Dad.

"Yes, if he's alive, that's the plan." Detective Lancaster nodded. "I'll let you get your rest, but please call me if you think of anything else or have questions."

Mom waited until the detective left, then she pounced. "I don't believe everything was fake between you and Aurora. Nor do I believe that she doesn't care about you and wants to break things off."

"Mom, I can't—"

"Maybe not right now, Kylian, but you must face how you feel about her. And if you love her, fight for her. No matter the lies she told to protect herself, she's a good person." She brushed some hair back from my forehead. "And so are you."

"I love you, Mom. And I know Aurora's a good person." But what we had wasn't real, even if Mom seemed to think it was.

"Back to your relationship being pretend. I'm not buying it. You care for each other. It could be that Aurora broke things off because of guilt, or that she's afraid her presence will bring you more harm."

My mind argued that I was a fool, that Aurora's part was an act and I had the proof in the form of a diamond in the palm of my hand. Everything had been built on a lie, which had only snowballed from there.

"You need to look at her actions."

"Mom—"

"Please try to keep an open mind. I hope you both work things out because I know how you feel about her. I witnessed it, and you can't lie to me. I just don't want you to throw this away."

"I'm furious." About her returning the ring, but I couldn't vocalize that. It was too painful. Instead, I used the obvious to hide my pain. "She didn't tell me the truth. About who she was, about her crazy ex-boyfriend. I would have been more aware. And while I was busy falling for her, she still didn't care enough to tell me. And that's fucking killing me." And that was before I realized I was just a meal ticket that could no longer pay off.

"Did you tell her how you felt?"

I scowled in response.

Mom laughed. "Despite what men think, we're not mind readers. Cut her some slack." She rested her hand on my arm. "Maybe you should ask yourself why you're so angry with her, and if that doesn't work, you should ask her why she didn't tell you everything. She has a valid reason, and you won't know until you talk to her."

Those words haunted me as the days bled together in a series of PRP injections and physical therapy. I worked my ass off, but the reason that had put me in the hospital was never far from my mind. Twelve days had passed, and the cops still hadn't found the fucker, if he was, in fact, dead.

CHAPTER TWENTY-NINE

KYLIAN

It was my first night back in my condo after recovering at Mom's for a month, and already, the guys were shooting me wary glances.

"Join us." Ares waved me over from where he and Liam sat in the living room.

After standing on the sidelines and holding a clipboard at practice, I'd stayed late to watch film and review a few findings about the opposing team with Coach. It was dark outside, and my stomach was trying to eat itself as I stood in the doorway to my room, having dropped my bag on the bed. "Sounds serious."

They waited until I sat on one of the club chairs before pouncing on a reoccurring topic since they'd heard that Aurora had returned my ring.

"I know what she did about the ring sucks. Trust me, we're team Kylian. But… we're also team Aurora. She's good for you, man, and I'm sorry if this comes across as harsh—"

"You need a wake-up call," Liam said.

Ares leaned forward, his mouth pulled in a disapproving slash. "We saw the way she looked at you, and that's not all. She went to your mom's and helped her—a lot."

"It's time to get over your hurt feelings and look at the bigger picture. So fucking what if she lied to you?" Liam huffed. "And before you say it, we know giving back the ring was shitty, but have you maybe thought someone else was making her? Or that it was based on guilt? You gotta get over the anger."

I got dumped by the woman I loved and thought I would lose my future career at the same time. It had been a lot to process. Depression had hit me hard. "I'm not mad at her. Not anymore." I ran my hands through my hair, wanting to push the guilt as far away as possible, but my roommates wouldn't let me. Goddammit, I missed her. I missed seeing her smile, the way she smelled, how we argued about football—which team was better —and how she'd slowly begun to trust me. That was the best gift she could've given me, and I'd gone and fucked it up by agreeing to see Melanie. I knew it, but I'd become a machine trying to get well and stave off the depression of what I'd almost lost for my future and Mom's. It had clouded what my endgame was. Not football, not really. It was Aurora.

"If she was reacting out of guilt, talk to her. If your dad got to her and threatened her directly, then do something about him. Blackmail him for a change. Something," Liam snapped. "You've had six weeks to fix things with her, and you haven't done a goddammed thing."

"She hasn't come around. She's done with me." Ever since she returned my ring, I hadn't heard a word from her, more proof that she meant it when she said she didn't care for me. It left an impression, and it had taken all I had to accept that fact.

"Can you blame her for running? It's what she does, right?" Ares's voice lacked heat, but that didn't stop his words from hitting home. "And if your dad did something… you know how ruthless he is. You gotta find out and fight for her."

I closed my eyes, for once, listening to what my roommates were saying. It wasn't as if I hadn't wondered the same thing. But throwing myself into recovery had been easier than picking at the raw wound after she dropped me, looking for a reason why.

"You need to snap out of it. Live again," Liam said. "Football can't be the only thing you let yourself care about in life. And it wasn't taken away, not fully. Besides, the asshole who fucked you up is the one to blame, not Aurora."

"Why do you care? You never date the same girl twice. Or not anymore." I could understand Ares being mad at me. *But Liam?* I didn't get it.

"First of all, don't go there. This intervention isn't about me." Liam's mouth twitched. "Second, she cooked for us. I want her back."

"You've got to be kidding me." I ran my hand over my mouth, struggling for words.

Ares cracked Liam in the back of the head. "She's not your live-in chef."

"I know." Liam shoved Ares's hand away. "But I liked her. And she was good for you." A wide smile stretched his mouth. "And the food was a bonus."

"Look"—Ares kicked his feet up on the coffee table—"we're concerned because you haven't reached out to Aurora to find out if she's okay. What if that fucker isn't dead? Have you considered that?"

I had to breathe slowly through my nose, fighting blind panic at the thought of that asshole laying a hand on her. "The detective promised he had cops watching the boat, where she's still staying. Mom's dropped off groceries and checked on her a few times. And they have DNA. They think he's dead."

"Why the hell is your mom doing what you should be?" Ares shouted.

"Because I'm doing my goddammed best to get my life in order. Do you think it's easy to recover and return to the game despite the odds against me? Or helping Calvin Fucking Matthews be better while he's in my spot, leading my team? Or being dumped by the girl I…" I couldn't finish that statement. It hurt too much. "She doesn't want me in her life. She made that clear the day she returned the ring to me."

"We know, man." Liam sighed. "It's bullshit. All of it. As for the football, Calvin is not you, and he'll never be, even with all the coaching in the world. You'll be back at QB1 at the start of next year, then it's on to the pros."

"You know we'll help you with whatever you need," Ares said. "Being captain of the team and trying to help Calvin be better is a tough spot, not to mention the hurdles you're overcoming post-surgery. Say the word, and we'll step in and smack that dumbass Calvin around. He's a useless waste of your time. No matter what you tell him to change to improve, he just doesn't listen. He's got too big of an ego."

"Seriously." Liam absentmindedly rubbed the scar on his left cheekbone he'd gotten from a fight freshman year with Maverick Davis, a hockey player who happened to be Calvin's cousin. "I wouldn't mind going toe-to-toe with Calvin, and maybe Mav will jump in again and defend his worthless cousin so I can have another shot at him."

"No fights." I felt a headache brewing.

"Or none that campus security can get word of," Liam amended.

Ares grunted. "We're getting off track. What're you gonna do about Aurora? Because you need to do something. Ignoring what happened or what you guys had won't help either of you."

"I appreciate what you're trying to do, but please, just stay out of it." I stood, went into my room, and slammed the door behind me.

Thoughts of Aurora swam behind my eyes. Her laugh, that gorgeous smile, when she finally trusted me and leaned into me rather than away as if something startled her. Her generosity with Mom.

I leaned against the door, and my head thumped against it.

Were they right? Did she break up with me because of guilt from what her ex did? Did my dad get involved and scare her away? Or did she show her true colors once she thought I could no longer play football?

CHAPTER THIRTY

AURORA

I sat cross-legged on the deck, the afternoon sun warming my shoulders on the unseasonably balmy day. The boat's gentle rocking soothed me in a way I'd never thought possible. It was home. I hated that I would have to leave soon. But it was about time to get on the road. For the moment, I enjoyed the relative peace while I worked on altering a recipe for the café on campus, where I'd found a part-time job.

It wasn't too difficult, since I loved to cook and the owner had given me some creative liberties with the menu. I wanted to be close to Kylian, even if I could no longer be with him.

I'd stayed on at the café in the hopes that I would run into him and maybe we could talk. I'd heard from his mom that he was back in school. And since I'd committed to the job, it felt right to see it through until the end of October—that was what I told myself. Then, I would figure out my next step. I missed him like crazy. I'd never thought that our business agreement would result in me wishing it was real. An ache throbbed in my chest at the thought because it had sure felt real. Or it had until his dad had made me put an end to it.

I'd spoken to Evalyn several times. She hadn't held it against me that I'd broken up with her son. According to her, I was suffering from misplaced guilt and the two of us would figure things out and get back together. She'd even asked if Kylian's dad had had a hand in it, which had terrified me. I hated lying to her, but if he found out I told her… I didn't even want to think about it.

I'd been in limbo since the cops hadn't found Dayton's body. However, they did find DNA from—*gross*—a severed finger. Both a blessing and a curse. I assumed he was dead, and so did the cops, but we all would feel better if more of his body were located. The part of me that wanted him to pay for everything he'd done to me and Kylian wished the body of water housed a giant crocodile. I would feel so much better about that. Waiting to find out if he was dead or alive was killing me.

If he was still alive, I was in serious danger. Especially since I hadn't left the boat. I wanted to stay there, despite the slight risk. It was where I felt close to Kylian, and I wasn't ready to give that up. Even if it meant Dayton would know precisely where to find me when he was ready—*if he's alive*. I chose to believe he'd died because, if he were alive, he would have come for me already.

"Knock, knock."

I followed the voice and smiled at Kylian's mom. "Evalyn, how are you? How's Kylian?"

She held a brown grocery bag in her arms, and I jumped up to help her get onto the boat.

"I'm fantastic, and Kylian is a machine. The only spare time he has between physical therapy, watching film, and class is to catch a few hours of sleep. I'd forgotten what a whirlwind he is when his mind is set to accomplish a goal."

"I'm sure he got that from somewhere."

"Flatterer." Evalyn laughed. "But yes, he gets some of that from me. Stubbornness too."

"Hmm." I didn't know what to say to that.

"I'm here to drop off some groceries and, ah, pick up some clothes for him."

Neither of us believed the fib about the clothes, but I didn't care. It was so good to see her. And I salivated to hear any tidbit about him because I couldn't get him out of my mind, no matter how hard I tried. "Thank you, and sure, grab whatever you need."

She paused, her gaze lingering on my face. "How are you?"

"I'm fine. Promise." I flashed a too-bright smile.

She wasn't buying it. "He's been staying with me, but it's probably time for him to return to the condo. I wouldn't be surprised if he sent me on a fool's errand, and he's already back there."

"Sure." *Is he really still at his mom's?* She'd hesitated over that part. I didn't believe her excuse for a moment, especially when it was accompanied by her wink. He had clothes at the condo and probably his mom's apartment too. *Why is she really here?* "So, his dad isn't causing any more problems about the condo?"

"No. Not that I'm aware of. I think his lawyer stepped in and straightened out his right to be there." She paused, her eyes sad. "Kylian asks about you often."

"Oh, ahh… that's so thoughtful, but you can tell him I'll be out of his hair and won't be here much longer." It was the truth. And I wouldn't let myself cling to the hope that he still cared. Not after how I left things with him. Though I wanted to stay on the boat, I had no right to remain. I'd tried to leave before, but I couldn't make myself go.

I could get a room in a basement apartment near the college. I didn't like the additional expense that would come with that, but it made sense. "The last thing I want is for something worse to happen to him because of me." Dayton could still be out there. It wasn't likely, but maybe. "I've already ruined his career."

I took the groceries from her and set them by my feet. She

sat next to me, a wistful grin curving her lips. She had more color than I'd ever seen on her face. It was promising. I wondered if something had changed. Mr. Wilder had said she was seeing positive results, but his word meant little.

"You did not ruin his career. It wasn't you who hurt him. And the doctors said that Kylian is making excellent progress. He has every reason to hope he'll throw a ball again. He just needs physical therapy and a little more time to heal, and he'll be back to where he was in no time."

"That's great news." I smiled, but I knew it was weak. It didn't change the fact that I'd brought danger to the table by accepting the fake relationship we had. On that, his dad was right. It would have been better for Kylian and everyone if I'd never climbed onto his boat. And he would be better off if I disappeared from his life.

"I know about the contract between you and my son."

"Oh." My face heated. "It doesn't matter. Without both of us wanting to honor it…" I shrugged.

I wouldn't make him stick to that, and verbally, I'd already released him from it. Besides, it wasn't legal. I hadn't signed the contract with my real name.

"Honey, you might be surprised by what Kylian wants to stand by, and you'll never know if you don't give him a chance to explain."

With that, she patted my arm, got to her feet, and hopped onto the pier. Her words stuck with me even after she was long gone. *Did Kylian tell her he wanted to talk to me?* I knew how busy his schedule had been before he got hurt, and it had to be even worse with all the PT and makeup schoolwork he had. *Plus, he would still be going to practice and doing some stuff, wouldn't he?* I imagined so, since it was such a huge part of his life.

I busied myself, putting the groceries away and straightening up. The day after the incident, I'd cleaned the blood off the floor and cabinets and even made some minor repairs. The place looked as if nothing horrible had happened.

Even with finding things to occupy my time after Evalyn left, I couldn't get what she'd said out of my mind, and I ticked through the list of reasons why I shouldn't see him.

It would be a risk. *But his bills had to have been paid by his dad for most of his recovery, right?* And his mom was doing amazing. *Could his dad still hurt them if I talked to him?* If Kylian's career did end before it even began, that would be my fault. Well, technically, it would be Dayton's, but I couldn't avoid some of that blame. Still, the need to speak with Kylian was suddenly overwhelming. Screw it. All those reasons should stop me from risking it, but they didn't.

I missed his smile, his strength, the way he took care of those who mattered to him, and all the times we'd talked. He could bring me to my knees with just a look or touch. With that reckless decision made, I hurried to shower and change into a sundress. I didn't have a car, so I called for a ride to his condo.

The entire time, I berated myself for such a rash decision. I would have no one to blame if he refused to see me and I had to spend an equally large sum to pay for a ride back to the boat.

My stomach was a bundle of nerves, and my palms were sweating as I thanked the driver and hopped out of the car in front of Kylian's building. When I pivoted to go toward the doorman, a flash of blond hair caught my eye. I jerked to a stop as Melanie Honeycutt—a.k.a. Science-Nerd Barbie—walked into his building.

I half turned, not wanting her or the doorman to see me or how much her being there hurt. Because I knew what that meant—he'd chosen her. I wasn't enough for him to fight for. What I'd done—who I'd brought into his life—was enough to sever any feelings he might have had toward me. It was all my fault. Sort of. Maybe.

A rush of pain shot through me, so much that my knees

threatened to buckle. I almost turned and fled. But I couldn't. I loved him enough to fight for him. Enough to tell him about his father blackmailing me to see if, together, we could find a way around it. I straightened my spine. We had something unique, and I had to try to make things right one last time.

Decision made, I hurried toward his building just as the fine hairs on my arms and along the back of my neck rose. Dread pooled as I got the eerie sensation that someone was watching me. Worrying it was the press, I scanned the area. My gaze hitched on the tall blond man across the street, just out of sight of the doorman, looking directly at me. My stomach churned, and I had to swallow several times to avoid throwing up from the combination of fear and the need to run. I had my answer—Dayton was alive. And he'd come for me. But instead of running, I changed course and walked toward him.

CHAPTER THIRTY-ONE

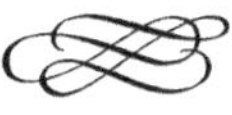

KYLIAN

Could this day get any worse? I stood at the island across from Melanie Honeycutt. With her index finger—I was surprised it wasn't her middle one—she pushed her black-rimmed glasses higher on her nose. I'd only opened the door because I was surprised by her appearance. It was a mistake to let her inside, and I knew that by the big envelope she'd slapped onto the counter.

Her blond hair was pulled up in a messy bun, and her black-framed glasses gave her a sexy-librarian vibe. Didn't matter, though. I felt nothing. All I could picture was what Aurora would look like with her dark-brown hair like that, wearing a pair of those glasses and nothing else. *Fuck. Why won't she get out of my head?*

The door opened, and Ares entered. Liam followed, and the door slammed shut behind him. Neither looked pleased at seeing Melanie. That made three of us.

"Saw Aurora at the café." Ares went to the fridge, ignoring Melanie as he grabbed food to make a sandwich.

I read the disapproval loud and clear. Liam sauntered up to Melanie and threw an arm around her shoulders as he whistled under his breath. "What have we here? You came to see me, didn't you?"

"Get off me, ape." Mel shoved at Liam.

He moved aside only because he wanted to. She was more like a gnat trying to move a mountain.

"I have no interest in anyone other than Kylian. And that brings me to why I'm here." She shot a pointed look at my roommates. "If we could have some privacy, please."

"This is a mistake." Liam rapped his knuckles on the island before he headed to the couch and the remote, ignoring Mel's eye roll. "Make me one, too, Ares."

"Already did." Ares grabbed the sandwiches and followed Liam but not before shooting me a disapproving look.

I got it. They were team Aurora, despite everything that'd happened.

"I still don't know why you're here, Melanie," I said.

"Look"—she rubbed her temples, briefly closing her eyes before she pierced me with a direct, no-nonsense hit of whiskey eyes—"you seem intelligent enough for me to lay all the cards on the table. I don't want to marry you any more than you want to tie your life to mine. But my dad has something on me."

"What are you talking about?" I focused on her like she was a wide receiver going for a long pass with seconds to throw before a defensive blitz.

She slapped her hand on the manila envelope she'd brought, the sound cutting through the banter between Ares and Liam while they played video games. "This."

I reached for it, and she snatched it away and cradled it to her chest. "Not so fast, hotshot."

"What the fuck is it with the stupid names? You've been hanging out with my pops, haven't you?" Red coated my vision. I was so sick of being played by my old man. "Are you sleeping with him? Is that the real problem?"

"Yeah, that's a hard pass and wrong team altogether."

"What?" I didn't follow, and I pinched the bridge of my nose between my fingers to ease the headache coming on. "Let's get to the point. You were all over me at the fundraiser." The reminder of our dads put me over the edge, and I was reaching for any argument I could find. "You come in here guns blazing with wedding prep"—I motioned to her envelope—"for a marriage I have no intention of going through with."

"Same page."

I ignored her. "And whatever this is"—I motioned again to the envelope she held protectively to her chest—"you're now saying you've been coerced into the same bullshit relationship that my dad is pushing with me? You're not making sense, so please, cut the crap and tell me what's going on."

"I'll need something to drink before I unload my life on a stranger."

"Coffee?" I reached for a pod in the canister on the counter behind me.

She scoffed. "No. Something much stronger. Do you have any Patrón?"

I grabbed a bottle from the corner cabinet along with a lowball glass and handed both to her. I blew out a breath, working to control my irritation. It wasn't her fault I wished it had been Aurora at the door and was disappointed when it wasn't. "Thanks for the flowers," I said, trying to ease some of the tension between us by acknowledging the gesture.

"What?" Her brows furrowed. "I didn't send you flowers."

"Huh, never mind." More manipulation from dear old Dad. He had to have sent them.

She poured two fingers and slung the shot back, her eyes closing as it went down her throat. I saw the appeal. She was gorgeous and connected and would probably make someone a great wife. She would understand the drive to succeed from growing up in a high-power world like she had. But she wasn't for me. And the more I understood who was, I realized what a fucking dumbass I'd been with Aurora. I should have fought for her, for us.

"Pass that bottle over here, Blondie!" Liam shouted from the couch, a devious grin curving his mouth.

"Get it yourself." She mumbled something unflattering under her breath that would only be a challenge Liam couldn't resist if he heard it.

He didn't really want the liquor. He was just messing with her. I caught the shade my best friends threw our way occasionally while they pretended to be engrossed in their video game. They'd been all over my ass ever since I'd told them everything about what had happened between Aurora and me. And I got it. Mistakes were made. Not only on her behalf—and she had a legitimate reason—but I hadn't appropriately prepared her for the steamroller that was my dad or listened to her when she'd said she didn't want anything to go public. And after seeing the consequences of her ex finding her, I understood why.

I was the one at fault and needed to rectify things between us. If I didn't, I could lose her for good, which scared me more than losing my shot at an NFL career.

Mel snapped her fingers in front of my face, and I growled at her. I wanted her out of here. "What?"

"If we want a way out of this, I need you to pay attention."

I caught her mumbling, "Fucking football players," and narrowed my eyes.

"Then get to it, so you can get the fuck out," I said.

After another eye roll, she set the envelope in front of her but kept her palm over it, French-manicured fingernails spread wide. "My dad is a right-wing extremist. He doesn't believe in abortions, gay marriage rights, or anything liberal. That being said, he's deeply ashamed of my preferences—"

"Which are not men." I'd finally caught on to her problem. It seemed I wasn't the only one being played by a parent.

"Exactly." She splashed a finger of tequila into the glass and swirled it around before downing it in one gulp.

"What does he have as leverage to get you to marry me?"

"My trust fund." Her full lips turned down, and she looked like someone had just kicked her puppy. "I was playing along because it's a lot of money. And I thought I could deal with his crazy scheme, marry you—"

"As your beard!" Liam shouted from the living room.

Melanie sent a sneer Liam's way. "And continue my life however I wanted. But… it's not worth my happiness."

"Just your happiness?" Banked anger burned hot under my skin, but I refused to give it free rein. I sensed a solution to our problems, and I supposed it was in the envelope she'd brought.

"Fine. You, too, I guess."

Ares snorted.

"I don't know you, like, at all, so your feelings haven't factored in as much as my messed-up dilemma."

I glanced at my nosy roommates, who weren't even pretending to play their video game anymore. Frankly, I could use the support. "Let's go in the other room." I left the kitchen to join them, and she had no choice but to follow.

"So, you're willing to ruin his life for access to your trust fund?" Liam started immediately.

"I'm guessing your girlfriend isn't too happy about it," Ares said. "Bet you can kiss that relationship goodbye." He tossed a handful of salted almonds into his mouth.

"Maybe she isn't worth it to you, but Kylian's fiancée is, and you've been fucking that up ever since you forced your way into his life."

I mentally high-fived Liam for that. "Why not hire a lawyer for the trust? You might be able to fight him and get it released."

"That's what my girlfriend said. Since Samantha is a paralegal, she has access to high-powered attorneys who can answer some questions. I've asked her to look into it, but in the meantime, I wanted to fill you in on what I know about our dads and what's driving them to push for this marriage."

"What do you know that I don't?" I was all ears.

"Our dads' campaign and development deal of the century is based on that old saying, 'Keep your enemies close.'"

"They've done business together before." It was starting to make sense. "I didn't know they had a development deal in the works."

"Yes, on both counts. The business they were previously involved in was a shady deal from about twenty years ago. They were business partners and scammed their investors out of millions of dollars when the deal went belly-up. It was almost a scandal, and my father paid a boatload in hush money."

"So that's why they're both pushing so hard on the marriage. It connects them on another level."

"That's a warped viewpoint," Ares injected. "Thinking that marrying you two will keep the other in check."

"Exactly," Mel answered. "But their egos must think it'll work."

"Sounds like they're cut from the same cloth." Liam leaned back on the couch, his arm extending along the cushions.

"That works in our favor. If they don't recognize that they're the same person, we can leverage the information against them. We have it, right?" I tapped the envelope, and her fingers curled tightly around the edges.

"We do."

"I'll need to see that."

She shrugged. "I'll show you, but I'm keeping the original copy. It's my insurance to fight against him. I'm only letting you in on it so you can do the same on your end. I don't know what your dad has over your head, but it must be just as bad, if not worse, for you to agree to their scheme."

I wasn't going to share about my mom. I nodded instead. "He's got enough leverage to work with."

She flipped the envelope and lifted the flap before pulling out several papers. "This shows the business name"—she tapped her nail against the appropriate place—"here. You can see both of their signatures. If you follow the shell company's history, that's where things get more interesting. I have digital copies of as much as I could find, some from the internet."

"What will you do with it?" My mind raced, and a plan began to form. But I wouldn't do anything until I talked things over with Mom.

"I'm still deciding. It might depend on what Sam finds out from the trust lawyer she's been talking with for me. I need bank statements, an account, something, and I don't have it. What I have is damning enough, but will it take them down for good?" She shoved the papers back into the envelope then stood. "All I ask is that you keep me posted, and I'll do the same."

I couldn't pass up the opportunity. "I want copies."

She handed over the envelope. "That's what these are. I wanted to make sure you were as invested in stopping them as I am before I gave them to you."

"Trust me, I'm all in, and I'll keep you updated. I might be able to find the missing data we need." I walked her out then turned to find smirks mirrored on Ares's and Liam's faces.

It was Ares who spoke, saying what we all thought. "She handed you a get-out-of-jail-free card."

"Take advantage of it, and go get your girl." Ares slapped me on the back.

They weren't kidding. If my dad had any hold over Aurora, this was my chance to obliterate it. "Oh, trust me, I will, but after I talk with Mom and get her the hell out from under his thumb too." And maybe even gain access to additional evidence.

I spent the drive to Mom's thinking about the best course of action, and what made the most sense was a turnabout—blackmail. The worst-case scenario would mean handing over everything Mel had to the Federal Trade Commission or whatever branch of government handled fraudulent businesses.

I'd called to ensure Mom was home and hurried up the stairs as soon as I found a spot to park. She let me in at the first knock, worry clouding her eyes.

"What's this about? You sounded angry on the phone. Did you reinjure your shoulder?"

"No." I rotated it, feeling only a tinge of tightness. "It's about Dad."

Mom huffed out a breath, and her shoulders dropped. "Okay, let's talk about it."

We sat on the worn sofa, and I filled her in about everything. From the fundraiser and threats to do what he wanted or she would suffer when it came to both her living arrangements and the money needed for treatments to the pressure to marry Melanie Honeycutt that would only further his career. I finished with the information Mel had shown me.

"I'm tired of being beholden to him. Will you please move into the condo next to mine? I have enough to put a down payment on it, and when the NFL signs me"—*because dammit, I would be on a team*—"I'll pay it off."

"Okay."

I leaned back, surprised. "Really?"

"Yeah, it's time. I shouldn't be here if everything comes crashing down around him. And I have a feeling it will."

"You didn't seem surprised about anything I told you."

"I was about Melanie. I can't believe he would stoop to that level to control Honeycutt. But about the business dealings, I'm not. I have copies of the paperwork and offshore bank statements. I've used it all these years to make your father behave."

A feeling of determination and satisfaction spread through me because I knew exactly what to do.

CHAPTER THIRTY-TWO

AURORA

I knew what I was giving up and why. Defeat-infused nausea churned my stomach. *I can do this.* I forced myself to take each step away from Kylian's condo and toward Dayton instead, despite the way my body rebelled at the action. Dark clouds coated the sky, obscuring the sun. The threat of rain, thick in the air, had nothing on the dampness coating my palms. Saliva pooled ominously in my mouth. I swallowed frantically to quell the urge to vomit at what was in store for me.

The need to protect Kylian from my monster was greater than fighting Blondie and staking a claim on what I thought we could have. It would have been selfish. I had to save him from the danger that waited in plain sight. That was why I left the condo and went toward my worst nightmare. I owed Kylian, and more than that, I wanted him safe—even if it cost me my freedom.

In the very beginning of my relationship with Dayton, I'd thought I loved him. He was so handsome and wealthy, and I was shocked he'd shown any interest in me. We'd gone to the finest restaurants. His home was incredible, and I'd spent the majority of my nights there until he'd asked me to move in with him, which I'd done happily—albeit blindly. Over time, his control had eaten away at my self-confidence, and it wasn't long before I saw him for the monster he was.

Dark spots danced along the edges of my sight as it tunneled, and I latched my vision onto the banked fury simmering in Dayton's eyes. I was aware of his power play yet helpless to fight it. He let me come to him, and I gagged at the perverse pleasure at my expense, which curved the corners of his mouth in a sadistic smirk.

A few feet away, I stopped, unable to force myself closer. He bared his teeth, and a violent shiver rocked me onto my heels, but I refused to retreat, to let him win another battle.

"How did you survive?" He couldn't swim. It didn't make sense.

"Not well, bitch." He held up his hand, and I winced at the missing pinkie finger. "This is your fault. I couldn't go to the hospital, and it got infected. If it hadn't, you can be damn sure I would've taken back what was mine much sooner." Darkness swirled in his eyes. "You're going to pay for making me chase you, my fallen angel."

I cringed. The addition to his favored pet name hadn't escaped my notice. He used to call me "angel." The added "fallen" lent insight into my newly tainted status.

In a move too fast for me to react to or pull away from, he latched onto my wrist with a crushing, viselike grip. I swallowed a whimper at the pain radiating through my fingers and up my arm as he yanked me to his side. It was the same wrist he'd broken before, and I knew the brutal pressure he applied was a reminder to instill fear.

It wasn't necessary. I was terrified of what he would do when we were alone. I'd lived through that nightmare before. It was the reason I'd run. Now, I feared it would be what killed me.

I kept my mouth shut while he shoved me into a nearby car.

As he rounded the front of it, his eyes never left mine—daring me to make a break for it. But too much was at stake. It wasn't just my life in the balance. It was Kylian's too.

With his gaze locked on mine, Dayton rolled his full lower lip into his mouth, caught it with his teeth, and scraped across the flesh as he released it. He thought it made him look hot, sexy. In the beginning, it had, and I'd wondered how it would feel to have his lips pressed against mine. Until I'd found out.

Despite the car's cleanliness, the scent of tobacco and mint permeated the interior. His scent. My stomach clenched. I hated it.

He got in the driver's seat, the smell growing stronger with his presence, and started the car. As we drove, I systematically locked everything that mattered to me in a mental box. The only way to survive Dayton's moods and appetites was to become an emotionless shell.

When we stopped at a red light, his fingers cruelly fisted the hair at my nape. Like a rag doll, I went where he pulled me. His efforts to keep me present intensified the more I drew into myself. The feel of his nose along my neck sent a volley of unwanted goose bumps across my flesh. Sharp pain exploded along the sensitive skin by my pulse as his teeth nipped hard enough to bruise. It would be one of many.

He wanted to mark and own me. To punish me. And while he might control my body for the foreseeable future, I'd won. Kylian was safe. Dayton's focus was solely on me. That fact was what kept a tiny spark of satisfaction and hope alive. It would have to be enough. Without it, I didn't know if I could mentally survive what was coming.

When the light turned green, he released me, and I shifted against the door. It was temporary. I wasn't out of his reach, and based on his anger, he would keep me close.

In the distance, thunder rumbled. I wanted to will the storm closer, for lightning to strike the car. Piece by piece, I hid more of myself, huddling in a corner of my mind, just like I did against the passenger door. The pain he inflicted when it amused him dulled my thoughts elsewhere. I spun a web of fantasy, retreating to a moment when Kylian had touched me.

I had the time, and what better way to transport my mind than to go back to the beginning. Kylian had exhibited kindness toward a stranger. Looking past the invasion of his property to the person, not the crime. He saw someone in need and reacted. Sure, our arrangement was mutually beneficial, but he didn't have to help me. He'd given me a way to accept his handout with pride.

I basked in how safe he'd made me feel—how my ability to smile and laugh had returned. The longer we were together, the faster I'd fallen for him. Though I'd tried to bow out of his life so I didn't complicate things further, I'd never wanted to.

I recalled the first brush of his lips, the way he'd slanted his over mine, deepening the kiss, my body lighting on fire for his. I escaped into what it was like to be in Kylian's embrace for as long as I could until Dayton pulled me back to the present during our drive. But I had practice escaping reality—my small rebellion—and used every ounce of my strength to transport myself elsewhere.

The door wrenched open, violently tearing me from the past, and I fell backward with a shriek. Dayton grabbed my upper arm. Fingers bit into my bicep, stopping me from crashing to the cement. He dragged me from the car, and I stood on shaky legs, orienting myself as quickly as possible.

The harbor? Shock momentarily stole my words until the pieces fell into place. It wasn't over. I'd thought I was saving Kylian, but I'd condemned us both.

CHAPTER THIRTY-THREE

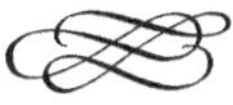

KYLIAN

The storm worsened as I sat in Dad's Chicago office. Lightning pierced the sky in a backdrop behind his thirty-something administrative assistant, who kept flashing me apologetic smiles. My father had kept me waiting for an hour. Each minute that ticked by only served to harden my determination and add another log to the banked fire inside me. I was ready to kick his self-righteous ass.

I was about to jump out of my skin, my foot tapping to expel some of the excess energy. He was going down. The days of him controlling Mom and me like puppets were almost at an end. I was armed with information and proof that he couldn't slither out from under. And I didn't feel bad about throwing him to the wolves.

Hours before arriving, I'd shared the data from Mom with Melanie. Immediately after, I'd contacted the FBI and the Illinois Attorney General. The number I was to call was already preprogrammed into my phone. A buzz sounded, and every nerve ending in my body zapped with the need to move.

"You can go in now," the secretary said with relief as she gathered her belongings, signaling the end of her workday.

I slid my hand into my pocket and pressed the button to connect the preprogrammed number as I grasped the brass doorknob. A turn and push of the door revealed Dad, dressed in a charcoal-gray suit with a white button-down and red tie, sitting behind an ornate desk. A bookcase behind him displayed tomes and pictures of him posing with various members of Congress and other high-powered businessmen, the perfect backdrop for meetings.

He leaned back in his chair, not bothering to stand, and waved for me to sit across from him, like a goddammed king. I shouldn't have been surprised. There was no love lost between us. And soon, our relationship would dissolve to irreparable levels.

"Kylian, what a nice surprise." Dad flashed a practiced smile. "I just wish you would have called. I could have had my administrative assistant pencil you in to avoid waiting."

"And give you an opportunity to be in Springfield instead? No thanks, I've played that game before."

I knew how he liked encounters with Mom and me—on his terms. And though I was on his turf, he didn't like surprise visits containing issues he wasn't optimally prepared for. Not that a snake in the grass like himself couldn't outmaneuver his opponents, even in a surprise face-to-face.

Anger flashed in his eyes, but he never let the emotion color other aspects of his practiced persona. "What's this about? Did you get some bad news from the docs? Don't tell me your NFL career is compromised."

For that, I let some of the irritation slip. "No. I'm good. Nothing to worry about there. You still have bragging rights." *For now.*

"Then, to what do I owe the pleasure of your company?"

"I came across some rather disturbing information about you and a land deal where you cheated people out of their hard-earned money. Since you've used every tactic to control Mom and me, this tidbit flips the tables in our favor." And it was about goddamned time.

He leaned forward, and I mimicked his pose, careful not to compromise my phone's speaker.

"Your mother finally told you all the details?" He pensively rubbed his fingers over his top lip. "I wondered why she hadn't done it sooner. After all I did for her when we were married and just starting out, and now, with the free rent and covering her astronomical medical bills."

I wouldn't go there. He used me anytime Mom or I needed help. "Good thing you already paid up for the next two months with the news coming out."

He huffed. "I don't know what you're talking about, Kylian. I have nothing to worry about. All the paperwork you're referencing is public knowledge. I have nothing to hide."

"The real accounting books are out there."

"There's no proof. Everything from twenty years ago is erased, gone."

"Oh, Dad, rookie mistake. Don't you know the internet is forever?"

He stood, towering over me, which I couldn't allow.

I uncurled from my chair and matched his six-foot-three height. "I have names, dates, and a money trail that links you to Honeycutt and the scam. You'll have to repay the money and possibly face jail time."

"That money never existed. It's all smoke and mirrors." His tone turned threatening. "The apartment building your mother lives in is built on that property. You do anything, and she'll suffer."

"As of two hours ago, she doesn't live there anymore." I'd enlisted Ares and Liam to help move Mom, and we'd gotten everything done by maxing my credit cards. We'd left the furniture behind. It was all beyond old, and I'd made sure she had a new set, soon to be delivered. I paid extra for the bed to arrive that day. "I've made sure you can never threaten her again. Your accommodations inside a federal prison won't allow it."

"I see I've taught you well. It's a good bluff."

He looked proud, and I almost vomited in my mouth. What a sick, twisted fuck. I estimated the time. Another arrest should be happening currently. "I'm nothing like you, and I'm not bluffing. Turn on the TV. A news break should be showing the feds hauling Honeycutt out of his office building in cuffs right about now."

When he didn't move for the remote, I went to the credenza on the far wall, pressed the control's power button, then turned the station to the appropriate channel and turned up the volume. Sound blasted through Dad's office as a reporter narrated footage of a cuffed Honeycutt being led from his house by the feds.

Dad remained frozen while the reporter's voice detailed the events as they unfolded. "Authorities have received new information about a land scam perpetrated twenty years ago by Harland Maxwell Honeycutt and another investor not yet named by the authorities."

Instead of watching the TV, I observed the color leach from Dad's face. He had seconds of freedom left.

"I'm not worried about that. The fool probably incriminated himself somehow. It's good you didn't get mixed up with Melanie."

"She has nothing to do with this." I needed that on record, not that she required saving but because I wouldn't let him taint anyone else on his fall from power. "You don't have much time. I need you to know that Mom and I are done with you. Our connection is severed as of this moment."

His lips peeled back, and he sneered. "You've got nothing on me."

The office door burst open, and agents swarmed inside. I stepped back, giving them more room.

Dad spat a parting threat my way as the officers read him his rights while slapping cuffs on him. "This isn't over, *son*. I'll be out by dinner."

That might be true, but it would be a long time before he could wreak havoc on any life but his own, and that was all I cared about. Well, not all.

I'd needed to make things right because I'd figured out something vital—Aurora was my endgame.

CHAPTER THIRTY-FOUR

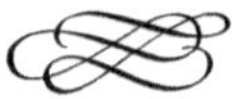

AURORA

The first hit came out of nowhere. Dayton cupped the side of my head and slammed it into the wall as we descended into the sailboat's cabin. I should have expected it, but I'd grown soft. The white-hot fear I'd lived with for so long had faded due to how safe I'd felt in Kylian's presence.

I'd had a slight reprieve as darkness surrounded me. But I wasn't unconscious anymore, and it wouldn't be long before he realized that. I used the gift of time and cataloged my surroundings. My hands weren't bound, and I was still wearing clothes—small favors. I ignored the intense pounding in my head and waves of dizziness.

The softness beneath me meant I was lying on a bed, but the sound from the TV told me I wasn't in the primary bedroom. Dayton probably didn't like the idea of Kylian and me sharing that bed. He wouldn't go anywhere near it.

I didn't hear Dayton—but I felt him looming over me. A fresh wave of terror washed through me. I opened my eyes, my fear realized when a slow grin curved Dayton's cruel mouth.

"Welcome back to the living, my little fallen angel."

He brushed some of my hair behind my ear, and bile climbed my throat. I lurched up and hurried to the far end of the bed.

Mistake. He despised rejection. With a roar, Dayton slammed his fist into my face. Pain exploded in its wake, and a metallic taste coated my tongue.

A whimper escaped my swollen, bloody lips. Dayton didn't like it when I made a sound while he was punishing or "teaching" me. My cry of pain ignited another wave of fury. He grabbed me by the hair, yanking me off the bed. I scrambled with my hands and feet to stand or at least keep up with him to relieve the pressure on my scalp. I tripped and fell behind him as he dragged me into the main room before releasing me.

I hit the floor and swallowed the cry that stretched my throat to uncomfortable degrees. One second then another, and I flattened my hands on the floor and pushed myself up. On my feet, I held my position, waiting to see what he would do.

"Why are we here?" Bitterness coated my question.

I hadn't expected to end up on Kylian's boat. I'd surrendered to Dayton so he would take me far away from Kylian, back to where we'd come from—Dayton's stomping grounds. It was where he wielded the most power. His money had a long reach, though. *But for how long?* He couldn't have as many allies in Chicago willing to bend the law in his favor as he did in California.

I braced myself for whatever came next. He hated being questioned unless it was a chance to boast about his brilliance. And I suspected now might be one of those times, especially when the next hit didn't come.

The blond Adonis swung his gaze my way—such evil lurking behind a pretty package. I hadn't seen the rot he hid until it was too late, and I bet he'd fooled plenty of other unfortunate women. That was why it had taken me time to trust Kylian. But witnessing how he treated his mom had tipped the scale for me. It was a gift I didn't think I could ever have again—trusting a beautiful man. But for the short while we'd been together, Kylian had shown me I could.

"Aurora?" Evalyn called from the deck.

No! She couldn't be there. I took an unsteady step forward, and the room spun dangerously. "I'll make her go away," I told Dayton as I stepped toward the stairs leading above deck.

He yanked me close and whispered, "Call her down. We can use her."

We? As if we're on the same team? "No."

A cruel glint flashed in his dark eyes right before he back-handed me. I crashed into the banquette, and I couldn't swallow the cry of pain as my hip hit the corner.

"Aurora?" Footsteps hurried across the deck, then the door opened.

"No! Go away!" I shouted.

Dayton grabbed me by the throat, his fingers digging into already-bruised flesh. Cold steel pressed against my temple. "Shhh."

I opened my mouth to scream another warning, but his grip stole my air just as Evalyn appeared on the stairwell, the door clicking closed behind her. Her deep-blue eyes, the same as Kylian's, took in the situation within seconds. Her lips formed an O at the sight of the gun Dayton held to my head.

"Hello, Ms. Wilder. So good of you to join us." Dayton's fingers eased, and I gasped painfully for air. "Won't you have a seat?"

I rushed forward to block her, but Dayton's suddenly tight grip in my hair yanked me back. Evalyn closed the distance between us, her hands stretching toward mine, but he drew me to his side.

"This won't solve anything, young man." Evalyn's voice was stern, her features shuttered.

"Oh, but it will." Dayton laughed, the sound dark and disturbed. "Have a seat, or my sweet angel will suffer... more."

Evalyn did as he asked, and fat tears rolled down my face. This wasn't supposed to happen. They should have been safe. But I was a fool. I'd sacrificed myself for nothing. I should have called the cops then run. At least then he would have chased me, but the Wilders wouldn't have been involved.

A drawer opened behind me, and Dayton shoved a thin rope into my hands. "Tie her up."

I shook my head, tears coming faster, blurring my surroundings.

Dayton grabbed the back of my hair and pulled me close, his breath fanning the side of my face. "Do you need another lesson?" With his free hand, he caressed my wrist, the one he'd broken when I'd disobeyed him on another occasion.

I pleaded with my eyes for Evalyn to escape. I didn't want her to suffer. She already had from her illness, so goddammed much. I hated what I'd brought to her and Kylian's doorstep.

"Go ahead, Aurora," Evalyn said. "It'll be fine."

Pressure circled my wrist until I cried out, and Evalyn half stood.

I held out my other hand to stop her. "Okay." *Stop.* "I'll do it." I mouthed, *I'm sorry*, before gently wrapping the rope around her wrists. It wasn't enough, though. I had to keep Dayton distracted so he didn't see how loosely I tied it. "What do you want, Dayton?" I tried to infuse my voice with steel, but it was difficult. I craned my neck to look at him over my shoulder.

"I want what I always have—you. And to punish anyone who stands in the way of that."

"Evalyn isn't a part of this. And you're way off the mark if you think Kylian cares about me. He won't stand in your way. He'll probably pay for the plane ticket to get me to leave." I suppressed the shiver that threatened to broadcast my emotion. I hated talking like that in front of Evalyn, but I had to speak the same language as Dayton if I had any hope of getting him to listen. I needed him gone before someone, namely Evalyn, got hurt.

"She's the bait to lure your mistake to us."

I ignored what he said, needing answers and a little more time to make sure she could quickly get out of the rope without it being evident to Dayton. "How did you find me?"

"The picture online."

"I blocked my face in those." I knew I had. *Could one of the reporters have gotten a picture I was unaware of?*

"It was the daisy tattoo on your wrist. You showed it while trying to hide your face from the camera. When I saw that, I knew it had to be you. Your mom's name, Gia, was done in script in one of the petals. Imagine my surprise when I learned that's the name you were using."

How had I not noticed that when I saw a picture of myself online? The answer was simple. I'd been complacent. Stupid. And look where that had gotten all of us.

I finished tying Evalyn up and turned so I stood in front of her. Then I heard the keypad beeping. *Oh, God.*

Dayton's arm extended, the gun pointing at the spot where Kylian had to be standing.

"Duck!" I screamed, hoping he got out of the way.

The door swung open. Dayton fired a shot through it then grabbed my arm and pulled me in front of him. Time stood still as we waited. Evalyn whimpered behind me.

I couldn't look away from the stairs. When Kylian didn't walk down, I assumed the worst—he'd been shot. My entire body shook. I wanted to scream and cry, beat against Dayton until he was a bloody pulp. I did none of that. I had to think about Evalyn too. If I couldn't save her son, I had to at least try to help her.

Before I could wrestle myself free, Dayton dragged me up the stairs and to the door, where Kylian stood off to the side.

"Don't try to be a hero." He shoved the door wide and

pushed me to the side so his gun led the way. As I stumbled onto the deck, Kylian yanked Dayton away.

Our eyes met before Kylian wrestled Dayton for the gun. I knew what I had to do and raced back down the stairs as another shot rang out. *Please, don't let him get hurt.* Dayton, I didn't care about. I hoped Kylian had the gun and had shot him, but I was terrified it was the other way around.

My heart pounded against my ribs as I dropped to my knees and helped Evalyn get free. "Call 911."

She leaped up, pulled open a drawer on the other side of the small fridge, and handed me a wrench with shaky hands before taking her phone from her purse. A steady stream of tears ran down her face.

"Be safe." I didn't wait for her to call the cops. I raced back to the deck with the makeshift weapon she'd given me. I stumbled up the stairs, my free hand slapping against the deck as I pushed off it and stood, wrench at the ready. My eyes swept the area then widened when I spotted Dayton sprawled at Kylian's feet, unconscious. Blood trickled from a cut on his lip, and redness along his jaw appeared to be a bruise forming.

The wrench slipped from my grasp and clattered to the deck. Then I was face-to-face with Kylian, cataloging him for injury. A sob of relief breached my lips despite how hard I tried to keep it in. The sight of him made my knees weak. As they buckled, he grabbed me. Steel banded around my waist, holding me against his solid strength.

Rage lit a fire in his eyes as he gently touched my cheek. It didn't hurt too badly. "I want to end him for what he did to you," he said.

I shook my head, my grip tightening on his shirt. "I'm fine. Promise."

"You're not fine."

"I never meant for him to hurt you or your mom. I was leaving." I needed him to know I'd never meant for that to happen. It was my fault he and his mom had been in danger.

Evalyn appeared, and Kylian's eyes flared with fresh fury until she told him she was okay. Then I felt the full force of his focus, and nothing else mattered.

He touched his forehead to mine and took several deep breaths. When he got control, the fury was banked in his gaze, and a slow, wicked grin curved his kissable lips. "You can't go. You're still under contract."

My brows furrowed. "I don't understand." And I didn't. *After everything—Dayton, his injury, and even his dad's manipulation... how could he want me anywhere near him?* "I only complicate things." That was putting it mildly.

"I've kept my end of the deal"—he spoke as if I hadn't brought up a valid point—"but I would like to propose an addendum. We date for real this time."

CHAPTER THIRTY-FIVE

KYLIAN

I wanted to inflict as much damage as I could on Dayton all over again from what he'd done to Aurora. Her lip was swollen and cut. Bruises marred her graceful, slender neck. That wasn't all. One eye was almost swollen shut, and a bruise on her cheek mottled her beautiful skin. I wanted to kill him for how he'd hurt her.

Mom assured me he'd never touched her. To be sure, I scanned her for marks as she leaned against the mast. I didn't find any, but he'd scared her, and that was enough for me to want to commit manslaughter—to avenge Mom and Aurora.

By some miracle, I maintained control and focused on what was important—making sure Aurora was okay and keeping her by my side.

"You really want to date me after all this?" Her hand swept in the general direction of Dayton's unconscious body.

Sirens wailed in the background, getting closer by the second. I didn't have much time to convince her before we would have to give our statements to the police. "I do. You know how I feel about you."

"But Melanie. I saw her going into your building. And what about your dad's threats?"

"I need to know… did my dad force you to stay away when I was in the hospital? Did he threaten you and make you break things off between us?"

Fat tears rolled down her cheeks, following in the tracks of the others. "Yes. I'm sorry. I never wanted to do that. I was there that day, when you were in surgery, but he found me before I could go to you. He said he wouldn't pay for your aftercare and that your mom would be kicked out of the treatment program if I didn't."

I pulled her close, careful of her injuries. She rested her cheek on my chest, and I held her to me. "My dad won't be a problem ever again." I would fill her in on everything later. The most important thing was making sure she didn't leave me. "I'm so sorry that he got to you and that I wasn't there to shield you from him. Not fighting for you, or realizing there were extenuating circumstances behind what you'd said and done was a huge mistake. One I won't make again. I should have fought for you, for us. I love you, Aurora. I don't want to spend my future with anyone else, if you'll have me."

"I-I love you too."

"I'll always keep you safe. I just want more with you, not a fake relationship, a real one. If you'll give that to me." I wanted her to know she had a choice. After witnessing what she'd lived through with her ex, all the pieces fell into place—why she'd reacted so vehemently against having our engagement made public, her difficulty with trust. I only hoped she would give us a chance. "I'm not your ex, or like my father. I promise you that."

She lifted her head, and our eyes caught and held. "I know that. I feel safe with you. I can be myself. It was never that way with Dayton. And well, your father… I just couldn't do anything more to hurt you or your mom."

"Will you give us a chance?"

A beat passed before she nodded. "Yes. I want to."

"Move in with me."

Her good eye widened. "But what about your roommates? Won't they mind?"

"No. They've been on your side the entire time." I laughed, thinking about how they'd made their opinions clear when I'd had my head up my ass after getting stabbed and letting her walk out of my life, believing what she'd said in the hospital when I should have seen through to the pain swimming in her eyes. I wasn't perfect, but I would do everything I could to make sure she was happy.

Blue lights flashed as two squad cars screeched to a halt in the harbor. The rumble of thunder in the distance vied with their sirens. Several fat raindrops splashed on our heads and the deck. Soon, there would be a downpour, and I wanted to get Aurora and my mom inside before that happened.

The police rushed along the pier as an ambulance pulled up. I forced myself to let go of Aurora so she could take a step back and speak with the officer. My hand slid down her arm, and I clasped her hand, reluctant to sever the connection entirely.

After we answered a few questions for the police, they slapped handcuffs on Dayton while reading him his rights. Aurora and Mom were escorted to the waiting ambulance and continued to give the police their account of what had happened while I did the same on the boat. I knew they wanted to separate us to ensure our stories added up.

As soon as we could put it all behind us, I would move Aurora into my place, and everyone I loved would be safe and in the same building. It was a sense of peace that I hadn't had in a long time.

In time, I would tell Aurora what I wanted for our future after a few years of playing in the NFL—a house and a couple of kids. I wanted a life with her, and as a bonus, Mom would get her grandchildren. It was the future I hadn't even known I wanted, but I did—more than anything.

CHAPTER THIRTY-SIX

KYLIAN

Two Weeks Later

I swept Aurora into my arms as soon as the door to the condo closed behind us. She clung to my shoulders, her legs automatically wrapping around my waist. My gaze shifted from her lips to her dilated eyes, and desire gut-punched me.

She was my every fantasy come to life. I spun her around, kicking at a backpack by my feet, then pressed her against the wall. Soft curves molded to my chest, and a burning need to have her erupted inside me. I slanted my mouth over hers. She opened willingly, melting against me, and I groaned at how good she tasted.

When she pressed against my chest, breaking the kiss, I growled.

A sliver of awareness sparked in her eyes. "Wait, what about your roommates?"

Fuck them. They needed to get gone if they were nearby.

"Ares, Liam, you home?" I shouted, never taking my eyes off her gorgeous face.

No one replied, and I'd never been so glad to have the condo to ourselves. "You drive me crazy. When you got up and leaned over to pick up that napkin, I almost bent you over the table right there in the restaurant."

She laughed and dropped her head to my shoulder. "The poor waitress. You growled at her to box everything up."

I'd taken her out on a date, one of many since we'd reconciled. "I don't care. It was worth bailing in the middle of dinner."

"Well"—she lifted her head and held my gaze—"you've got me alone now. What are you going to do about it?"

Not wanting to waste time or risk being interrupted, I crossed the kitchen and living room until I got to our bedroom. Kicking the door shut with my foot, I stopped at the end of the bed. She slid her legs down with excruciating slowness.

I peeled her clothing from her body, luxuriating in the softness of her skin and the full swell of her breasts. I didn't have much control left after watching her eat. All I could think of was feeding her my hard length and watching her lips close around me as she took me as deep as she could. But I didn't have the patience for that, maybe later.

"I won't go slow." I couldn't. Not tonight. Urgency to reassure myself that she was safe—and mine—fueled my every response. It'd been like that between us since the night I found her on the boat, bruised and bleeding from that asshole's fists. The desperation didn't come from me alone. She often reached for me, during the day and night. "Are you okay with that? We'll go slow for round two."

"You better go hard and fast." She tugged at my belt and worked the button free on my pants then the zipper. "I've been waiting just as long as you."

Fuck that. I tore off my clothes, needing to feel her skin against mine. Nothing would come between us. I ran my hands up her sides and around her chest then bent to tease, suck, and finally, bite the curve of her neck. She moaned as I rolled one nipple between my fingers then filled my palm with the plump weight of her breast. Her skin was like silk, soft and addictive.

When she threaded her fingers through my hair, I gripped the backs of her thighs and lifted until she wrapped her legs around me again. Her heat met my raging hard-on, and we groaned as I rubbed against her sensitive bundle of nerves.

Her hands roamed my shoulders, chest, and biceps as she ground against me. With her in my arms, I changed directions and took her back to a wall. I crowded her, pressing her against the hard surface. She tightened her legs around my hips.

"Still good?" I had to make sure.

"Yeah, stop talking. More action." Her breath mingled with mine, coming in short pants.

That was all I needed, and a grin curved my mouth. It fell away when she took me in her hand with a tight grip then a slow pump.

Fuck. I slipped my hand between us, dipping a finger inside her tight, wet channel. Her head fell back against the wall, her eyelids sliding shut as I pumped in and out. I slid another finger in, stretching her then curling them at the end until she squirmed in my arms. Her body squeezed me in a tight grip. She was close. I stopped moving, enjoying the feel of her. She was like a drug, and I couldn't wait to get my next fix.

Her wicked, heavy-lidded gaze met mine, and a corner of her full lips rose. "Get to it, QB1."

I swirled my thumb around her clit, and she whimpered.

"Stop teasing me. I want to come."

I needed to be in her like my next breath, and I slowly slid my fingers out as she shuddered against me. "Not yet." We had all night, and I planned to use every minute.

I shifted, still holding her suspended against the wall, and aligned the head of my cock with her entrance. In one thrust, I seated myself fully in her slick channel.

She cried out and arched her back, head falling against the wall as her nails dug into my shoulders. "So good." Her voice was breathy and sexy as hell.

Her warmth robbed me of all thought, and I dropped my mouth to her neck and teased her exposed tendon between my teeth. I held still until she squirmed against me. Then I pumped in and out as her body tightened around me. With each thrust, the connection I needed like my next breath, strengthened.

"I love you, Aurora. I never want to be without you."

"Kylian," she pleaded.

Moonlight from the window highlighted the sheen of sweat covering her gorgeous body. I worked to give her the release she craved. I picked up my pace, pumping in and out as she writhed against me. When I felt how close she was, I dipped my hand between us, swirling lightly over her clit until she screamed. Her body gripped me tight, and I followed her over the edge.

Her body went limp in my arms, and she whispered that she loved me too. I cradled her to me before making my way to the bed. I laid her down then went to the bathroom to clean up before bringing her a warm washcloth and doing the same for her. I tossed it to the floor, climbed in beside her, and pulled her to me so she could use my chest as a pillow.

As our heart rates regulated, I marveled at how perfect she was for me. I wanted to give her the world, and I knew I would stop at nothing until I did.

CHAPTER THIRTY-SEVEN

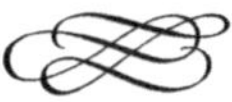

AURORA

Three weeks had passed since Dayton's arrest, and I finally had my life back. No threats hung over my head, and I'd taken a long look at what I wanted. It wasn't college. I'd kept my part-time job at the small café on Fall Lake University's campus, for the time being. A lot of soul-searching determined that I enjoyed cooking, a treasured time with my uncle, the most. He'd taught me everything I knew.

I'd toyed with getting a job as a chef in a few restaurants in downtown Chicago, but I wasn't sure that was the route I wanted to go. Kylian spent long hours with school, football, and watching film to prep for upcoming games. His drive and dedication were so admirable. I knew he would be okay with the long hours I would put in at a restaurant, but it didn't feel right. Maybe I would go the route of a private chef. I was still deciding.

I finished putting the last couple of meals I'd prepped for Kylian's roommates in the fridge. It had been fun adapting a meal plan for what athletes ate, and the guys showered me with compliments. That wasn't why I cooked for them. It made me happy, and after everything I'd lived through, I'd vowed never to let anyone control me again.

Kylian's mom loved the condo next to his. I'd helped decorate it and spent time with her often. We'd become friends, and I knew when Kylian and I moved, she would come with us wherever he was drafted. He and I were on the same page—life was short, and we wanted to spend it with those we loved. And the absolute best gift we'd gotten was that her cancer had finally gone into remission.

It was late, and the guys would return from practice and lifting soon. They had a big game the next day, and their coach had told them a few scouts would be there. Kylian had recovered, but he wasn't back on the field yet—he was slotted to start next August. With a little more time, it had become clear that the injury to his right shoulder would change nothing about his outstanding athletic ability on the field—because he'd worked hard to make sure of it.

I loved going to the games to support Kylian and his friends, and I couldn't wait for the next one. Well, I was excited about tonight too. We were going on a date, and he wouldn't tell me anything except what to wear, which was something comfortable.

The door opened, and Ares walked in, dropping his backpack near the door. "It smells amazing in here."

I grinned. "I just finished putting everything away. I thought you guys wouldn't be back for another thirty minutes." I peered around him. "Where are the other two?" It was still light out and would be for another hour or so.

"It's just me." A mischievous grin curved his mouth. "I'm supposed to take you to Kylian."

"Okay." That was new.

I went with Ares to his car. We drove for a while, chatting about classes and if he was dating anyone. He was not, something that always shocked me. Liam went through women like crazy, never to be seen with the same one twice. Ares was different. His drive and focus rivaled Kylian's. And something was going on with his home life that I hadn't quite figured out, despite meeting his mom and nephew. He kept things close. Sometimes, he would get a phone call and disappear without a word. I hadn't lived in the condo long. I suspected he would confide in me eventually. I hoped so. He and Liam were important to Kylian, which meant they mattered to me too.

"Are you guys ready for the game tomorrow?"

We had the home advantage against Michigan. I was surprised Kylian wanted to go on a date with me the night before a game. He wasn't playing, but he was always there for the team, on the sidelines, helping coach the stand-in starting quarterback. Friday nights weren't meant for staying out late, but I doubted we would be long anyway.

I'd become addicted to going to his games. It was so different from watching them on TV. I'd known he was extremely gifted, but seeing him in action, up close and personal before the accident—thanks to the fantastic seats I had—was on a whole new level. Even if I wasn't watching him, I loved the game and planned to cheer for the Fall Lake Ballers, especially Ares and Liam.

"Yeah, I'm ready. We all are." Ares drummed his fingers against the wheel while we stopped at a light. "There'll be scouts for teams actively looking for immediate positions to fill."

"Kylian told me. Not just for a quarterback, but one of the teams desperately needs a tight end. Or maybe it was the same team? I can't remember." It was a tough hit for Kylian, as he wouldn't be in the game. But I admired that he never let on that it bothered him because he was excited for his friends and teammates to have the opportunity.

"Coach didn't say. It would be amazing to be picked up at the same time as Kyl, but I'm still planning on doing the Combine." He grimaced. "I think any scout would be a fool not to pick him up early, injured or not."

The combine wasn't until February. The invitation-only NFL scouting combine was something Kylian planned on attending as well. He felt he would be in great shape to do so by then. I had no doubt he would get an invite.

At one point, he'd wanted to go straight into the NFL due to his mom's escalating medical bills. The new treatment—the one that had effectively put her cancer in remission—had been a constant source of stress for him.

We fell into a comfortable silence, each of us lost in our thoughts until we pulled into a parking lot, and I looked around, realizing he'd driven me to the harbor.

My heart rate kicked into overdrive. "What's going on?" I hadn't been back to the boat since Dayton's arrest.

Ares's topaz eyes widened when he noticed my utter panic.

"It's good. I promise. I wouldn't have brought you here if I didn't know you would like what Kylian had planned."

"He's on the boat?" I squinted, trying to make out Kylian through the fading light. I couldn't see him, but I spotted Liam approaching us.

"Yep. He's there. And I'm Liam's ride home."

"Okay." I flashed Ares a shaky smile. "I guess that's my cue to get out?"

Ares laughed and pulled me in for a quick hug. "I swear it's all good. I'll see you at home later."

My door opened, and Liam stood waiting with a similar grin.

"Hey, Liam." I didn't wait for them to say anything more. I took a deep breath, walked with purpose up the plank, then stopped short. Kylian stood on the deck, a table for two with dessert and candles set up.

He offered me a hand, and I put mine in his much larger,

calloused one as he helped me step on board. His big body crowded mine, and I felt a tug on my finger, but I couldn't look away from the intensity of his powerful presence. Then his hands were on my hips, and heat curled inside me at his touch. He looked slightly nervous, which only made me more so.

"Hi." I grinned. "What's going on?"

"I wanted a date with you tonight, and the guys agreed to help out."

"This is a lovely surprise." The setup was romantic, but he was acting strange. "Are you sure everything's okay?"

"Yeah, better than okay. I was going to do this later, but I can't wait. Our relationship—"

"Fake relationship?" I cocked a brow, trying to inject a little humor into the seriousness of his expression making me anxious. *What's he getting at?*

A grin curved his firm lips. "Yes, our fake relationship started on this boat, and I thought it would be fitting to take things to the next level here as well."

I was more confused than ever. I'd already agreed to date him when we were there last. *Oh... is he?*

Kylian dropped to a knee, holding the engagement ring I'd given him back in the hospital. "There's nothing fake about us. I think I knew you were the one the moment I saw you, even if I wasn't ready to admit that. At least I was smart enough to lock you into a contract."

An uncontrollable laugh escaped me. That was one way to put it, and I was so happy he had locked me into a legal entanglement. His expression turned serious, and I held still, waiting for what came next.

"You captured my attention from the start."

Another laugh burst from my grinning lips. "As did you."

He'd been naked, and there was no forgetting that swoonworthy sight.

He chuckled. "You're beautiful, Aurora, both inside and out.

You're my best friend. I look forward to everything we do together. You're the first thought in my mind when I wake up and the last one before I go to sleep. I can't imagine my life without you, and I'm so grateful that our paths crossed when they did. We've already faced incredible challenges, and through it all, we stayed together." He winked.

Mostly. I got what he hadn't said and grinned. I'd run when he'd tried to pressure me to announce our fake engagement. It was a terrible learned habit I'd broken—for him. I'd given my word never to do it again and would keep that promise.

"It's why I know that whatever life throws our way, we'll always come out on top together. When I go into the NFL and you pursue the career of your dreams, we'll make an incredible team. I love you, Aurora. I know in my heart that you're the one for me. Will you marry me?"

"Yes." Happy tears rolled free. "I love you, Kylian. Everything about you—your smile, your laugh, your fierce protectiveness, your dedication and drive. I can't imagine a day without you in it because you're also my best friend. You're the one for me." I fell into his arms.

At some point, he slipped the ring on my finger. Then his lips were on mine, soft at first then insistent. Everything faded, except how right it felt to be in his arms. That was where I was meant to be—with him. And I knew that no matter where we ended up, or whatever challenges fell into our path, we would be together—a team.

Thanks so much for reading my work. I hope you enjoyed it! As you know, an author's career is built on reviews. If you have a few moments, please consider leaving a review or rating for QUARTERBACK KEEPER.
https://store.amymckinleyauthor.com/pages/reading-order

Continue reading the Fall Lake Baller series with
Pump Fake.

211

ACKNOWLEDGMENTS

Thank you to all the incredible readers and bloggers for your amazing support. I couldn't do this without you! If you're not already on it, join my newsletter for updates on news and upcoming releases.

I am incredibly fortunate to have the most amazing critique partners, whose opinions and creative input have been invaluable to this journey.

Candace Irvin—thank you for being my constant sounding board, tirelessly reading and re-reading scenes, and offering insights that have shaped this story in ways I couldn't have imagined. Your friendship and support mean the world to me, and I'm so grateful to have you by my side.

To Emily Albright, Kristin Kisska, and Jessica Riley Miller — thank you for diving into the trenches with me, for your willingness to read these stories, and for your creative input, which has been instrumental in bringing this book to life. I am deeply grateful for your time, energy, and camaraderie.

I'm incredibly grateful to have Cass Thomasson with Chaotic Creatives and Colleen Noyes with Itsy Bitsy Book Bits in my corner, working their magic to make each release a success.

TE Black Designs consistently transforms my ideas into stunning covers, and the editors at Red Adept Editing are not only fantastic but also a pleasure to work with. I'm truly fortunate to have such an amazing team.

Thank you.

ABOUT THE AUTHOR

Isla Vaughn is the author of the Hidden Valley Elite and Fall Lake Ballers series. Her romance books are full of complex characters, strong alpha males, and the fierce women who bring them to their knees. When not writing, she can be found daydreaming about owning a beach house, reading, or drinking too much coffee.

facebook.com/author.IslaVaughn

instagram.com/islavaughnauthor

goodreads.com/islavaughn_author

bookbub.com/profile/isla-vaughn

tiktok.com/@islavaughnauthor

ALSO BY ISLA VAUGHN

Hidden Valley Elite Series

Savage Start

Savage Lies

Savage Truth

Brutal Days

Brutal Nights

Cruel Start

Cruel Hate

Cruel Love

Wicked Games

Wicked Ends

Fall Lake Ballers

Quarterback Keeper

Pump Fake

Red Zone

Isla Vaughn also publishes under Amy McKinley

Mafia Elite

No Way Out

Blood Oath

Born in Darkness

Savage Secrets

Ruthless Heir

Collateral Damage

Rivals

Verretti Crime Family (coming soon)

Borrowed Time

My Enemy's Bed

Fractured Lies

Gray Ghost Novels (Former Navy SEALs)

Moments That Define Us

Broken Circle

Eye of the Storm

Beneath the Surface

Vantage Point

Covert Threat

Marked for Death

Deadly Isles Special Ops (Navy SEALs)

Twisted Secrets

Bound by Secrets

Forged by Secrets

Standalone Titles

Shattered Melody

Siren's Call: Cursed Seas

Fake Fiancé (A Second Chance Office Romance)

Moonlit Destination Series

Moonlit Whisper

Moonlit Kiss

Moonlit Mirage

Five Fates Series

Hidden

Taken